"Are you trying to annoy me?"

"Is it working?" Ashley batted her lashes and sent sparks shooting off inside of Slade. "Try harder. I'm not shaking in my Gators."

"What makes you think I won't kill you?"

She made a sound that sounded like a snort, then seemed to catch herself.

"I'm a convicted felon. I've been given a life sentence."

"For what?"

"Murder. Three counts."

"Who did you kill?"

"Doesn't matter." A lie. He didn't want it to matter. For some reason, he didn't want her to know just how dark that side of him was. "It only matters that they're dead and I killed them. Just like I'll kill you if you don't do as you're told."

She smirked. "That might work on those guys, but it doesn't work on me."

He didn't have a response to that. No matter how fast his mind raced or how hard he thought.

"See? That. Right there." She circled a finger in front of his eyes. "I can see it. Shining, even as you try to hide it."

"See what?"

"A soul."

D0211630

Dear Reader,

I can't always pinpoint exactly where a story idea came from. In the case of *Prison Break Hostage*, however, the plot and characters burst into my mind during a road trip down to San Diego for a writers' conference with two brand-new friends. While "the Lindas" and I got to know each other, a prison bus passed us by. And this story was born.

Dr. Ashley McTavish doesn't stop. Not even when she should. Having a detective brother like Jack McTavish means she's always been prepared for everything. But she has absolutely no way of preparing for the roller-coaster ride one highway encounter creates, or her instant attraction to a convicted felon who takes her under his protective wing.

The last thing undercover agent Slade Palmer wants to do is take a hostage, but needs must. He's been working this case for two years and Ashley is trouble with a capital *T*. He's not a man easily thrown off kilter, yet Ashley seems to excel in everything she does. Slade soon learns what Ashley does best: she heals. Bodies and hearts.

I hope you enjoy this latest Honor Bound romance and that you fall as hard for Ashley and Slade as I did. I think they might be my favorite couple to date!

Anna J.

PRISON BREAK
HOSTAGE

———

Anna J. Stewart

HARLEQUIN

ROMANTIC
SUSPENSE.

HARLEQUIN®
ROMANTIC SUSPENSE™

Recycling programs
for this product may
not exist in your area.

ISBN-13: 978-1-335-75960-3

Prison Break Hostage

Copyright © 2022 by Anna J. Stewart

This edition published by arrangement with Harlequin Books S.A.

For questions and comments about the quality of this book, please contact us at CustomerService@Harlequin.com.

Harlequin Enterprises ULC
22 Adelaide St. West, 40th Floor
Toronto, Ontario M5H 4E3, Canada
www.Harlequin.com

Printed in U.S.A.

Bestselling author **Anna J. Stewart** can barely remember a time she didn't want to write romances. She's been a bookaholic for her whole life, and stories of action and adventure have always topped her list, especially if said books also include a spunky, independent heroine and a well-earned happily-ever-after. With Wonder Woman and Princess Leia as her earliest influences, she now writes for Harlequin's Heartwarming and Romantic Suspense lines and, when she's not cooking or baking, attempts to wrangle her two cats, Rosie and Sherlock, into some semblance of proper behavior (yeah, that's not happening).

Books by Anna J. Stewart

Harlequin Romantic Suspense

Honor Bound

Honor Bound
Reunited with the P.I.
More Than a Lawman
Gone in the Night
Guarding His Midnight Witness

The Coltons of Roaring Springs

Colton on the Run

Visit the Author Profile page at Harlequin.com for more titles.

For Lynda Bailey and Linda Hill.
Friendship forged on the highway.
This one's for you.

Chapter 1

Three hours and one minute. Dr. Ashley McTavish smothered a yawn and reached for the last of her stone-cold coffee. Just three hours and sixty seconds until she could sink into a nice hot bath and soak the last eight days out of her system. "Note to self." She leaned forward to peer into the black night through her windshield. "No more volunteering to cover for people you barely know." More like, no more being conned by a small-town doctor desperate for some alone time with his wife.

She was such a sucker for romance. Her dubious experience with it didn't matter; the thought just made her heart happy. After spending time with the charming sixty-something Dr. Fallon at a Northern California medical conference months before, she'd found herself offering her services so the good doctor could take his missus on a five-day cruise for their anniversary. She'd been new to the area and unemployed at the time. She'd needed to make professional contacts. Not that serving as the only doctor to fewer than two hundred people in a town so small she could have sneezed and missed it expanded her network. But she'd had some interesting visitors in the small Shasta Lake town and gotten her fill of fresh eggs, homemade pies and carb-laden casseroles.

Staring into the receding darkness off I-5, she wished she'd waited the few extra hours until dawn before heading out. The expansive overnight road construction on the main highway meant she was white-knuckling the unfamiliar, lonely drive. She didn't even want to think what these neglected roads were doing to the tires of her new SUV, but according to her GPS, she'd be home in—she squinted at the dashboard clock—two hours and fifty-nine minutes.

She'd enjoyed her time caring for Dr. Fallon's patients, and the slow pace gave her lots of time to catch up on her reading. Still, she missed her new job as the head of the emergency department at Folsom General. So much so she'd used her comfortable turquoise hospital scrubs at Dr. Fallon's clinic. But at least she wasn't going to miss Chloe Ann's christening. She couldn't wait to witness her brother, Jack, officially become godfather to Eden and Cole Delaney's infant daughter next weekend.

She tapped a button on the dimly lit dash screen and activated her phone. "Call Greta." Her new sister-in-law was a notorious night owl and Ashley needed something to keep her awake and alert since her coffee had run out.

The highway and back roads in this part of Northern California were known for their long stretches of boredom and lack of scenery, but at this time of night she may as well have been flying a ship in outer space, given the only good light came from the moon and stars. As Greta's phone rang, Ashley flipped her visor down to block against the oncoming high beams. She hadn't seen a car in miles. Nice to be reminded there was still someone else about despite the van's excessive speed as it whooshed past.

"This is Greta. My phone's either off or buried where I can't find it. You know what to do." Beep.

"Typical," Ashley grumbled. Her sister-in-law's attention was probably a thousand percent focused on painting a new canvas. "Hey, Greta, it's me. Just calling to check in. I'm on my way home now. I'm free for lunch tomorrow if you want to catch up and tell me all about the honeymoon." Ashley cringed. That sounded weird. She didn't need a lunch to know how her brother and his wife spent the last week and a half. She'd been married before. She knew how honeymoons worked. "Anyway, call me when you get a chance. Bye. Holy—"

A loud bang exploded ahead of her. The head-lights coming toward her swerved into her lane. In-stinct had Ashley aiming for the narrow shoulder. She hit the brakes and skidded to a stop as a dark-colored bus with Sheriff written in bright neon let-ters above the windshield shot past. She could see the driver struggling with the steering wheel as the bus went completely sideways. Ashley opened her window and leaned out just as the vehicle flipped. Metal pieces flew into the air as the bus rolled. Banging crash after banging crash exploding into the silent night. Glass shattered. Metal crunched. Smoke billowed out of the back of the bus as it slid to rest on its side, tires spinning.

Instinct and training kicked in. Ashley flew out of her car, raced around the back, and yanked out her emergency bag and flashlight. She ran full out, surprised at how far the bus had skidded. It was pure luck the bus had ended up directly under one of the sporadic streetlights. She could see deep black welts in the cement, could hear groans of pain, curses of anger. Cries of fear.

The rear emergency door on the bus burst open. Ashley dived toward it as two men stumbled out, the larger of the two clutching an obviously broken arm against his chest. The thinner, wiry man had blood streaming down the side of his face. Both were wearing bright orange prison jumpsuits. Both were handcuffed and belly chained.

The one with the head wound dropped to the

ground. He groaned and rolled onto his back, stared dazedly up at the stars before his lids drifted shut.

Ashley looked to the other man, who had braced himself against the back of the bus. "I'm a doctor. Can you walk on your own?"

"I'm okay," he croaked. He gestured to his friend. "Not sure about Clive."

Neither was she. She dropped down beside the suddenly still man, reached into her bag and snapped on a pair of gloves. She checked his eyes with her penlight, looking for pupil reaction. "He probably has a concussion. And that gash is going to need stitches. How many more are inside?" She didn't want to move this one until she had to. Darn it, she'd left her phone in the car. She dug around for the spare disposable she carried in her bag. No luck.

"There were six of us, plus two guards and the driver."

"What's your name?" She got up to check on him. "Javier. Javi."

"Hi, Javi, I'm Ashley. I'm just going to take a quick look at you, okay?"

"I'm fine." He pushed her hand away. "Busted arm. Had worse."

With no time to argue, she pointed to Clive. "You go over there with your friend, okay? I'll check on you both later."

She grabbed the flashlight, headed for the open door. The second she crawled inside, she was stopped by two firm hands on her shoulders. "You need to leave."

Ashley straightened, taken aback by the almost gentle quality of his voice. He was tall, well over six feet, and if he hadn't been a convicted criminal, he probably could have been an MMA superstar. She could see the outlines of tattoos on his neck, a scar arcing from temple to nose on the right side of his face and eyes the color of a summer sea beneath too-long hair. What the— Ashley attempted to shake off his grip. "I'm a doctor. I can help."

"Go. Now." He lowered his voice, leaned over her to the point she couldn't see, couldn't feel, anything but him. "Get in your car and drive away. You don't know what—"

"Lucky, Valeri's hurt bad, man. We gotta get him out! We gotta call Taras and get him back here! Man, oh, man. This is all going to crap!"

Ashley planted a hand on Lucky's chest and shoved. She may as well have been trying to move a mountain. "Out of my way."

"Lucky? You hear me?" A small man tripped and shuffled his way toward them. "Valeri's hurt."

"I heard you, Elliot." The rumble of Lucky's voice rippled through Ashley.

"Then what—" Beady brown eyes locked onto Ashley. "She a nurse?"

"She's a doctor." Ashley used Elliot to wedge herself past Lucky and clicked on her flashlight. "Who else is hurt?"

"Valeri's all that matters." Elliot scrambled around her, pointing at someone.

"I'm not anyone's private physician." She bent down beside the prone man.

"Look, Doc—" Lucky began.

Ashley shot to her feet so fast the man stepped back. "Tell me to leave one more time, I dare you." She moved in, looked up at him, eye to throat. "And it's Ashley. Or *Doctor*. Doc makes me sound like a soap opera heroine." Was it her imagination or did his lips twitch?

"Don't know why you're bothering with them," a uniformed officer yelled from the front of the bus. "They're bottom of the food chain."

"But they're first on my route," Ashley shot back. "Can you move everything?" she called to the officer, and at the same time bent over an unconscious man to assess his condition. His skin was glistening with blood. She pressed her fingers against the side of his neck.

"I can move," the guard answered.

"Good. Then get up and move out. Can someone get me some more—"

A light clicked on. She shielded her eyes, looked over her shoulder and found Lucky holding an additional flashlight.

"Put that down!" The guard yelled and reached to his side. An odd panic settled on his face.

"It's a flashlight, not a truncheon," Ashley snapped, continuing to search for a pulse on the unconscious man's neck. "And where are the keys to their restraints? They can't help if they can't move."

"Then they can't help." The guard seemed to still be fumbling for something.

Lucky bent down beside her and her adrenaline surged. She could smell sweat and blood. Along with tangy, metallic fear. Whether it was her own or his, she couldn't be certain.

"What's his name?" Ashley almost whispered, asking about the man she was treating.

"Dante," Lucky said. "We call him Inferno. He's gone?"

Ashley nodded, looked up at him. "I'm sorry."

"Dr. Ashley," Elliot whined. "Or whatever I can call you, would you please—"

"Tell me that one has a nickname," Ashley muttered and grabbed Lucky's flashlight.

Lucky's expression didn't flicker. "Badger."

"Fits. Once you get the others outside, please go and help the guard. Also, there's a phone back in my car. We need to call 911."

She didn't wait for a response before she moved deeper into the bus, the expansive beam of the industrial flashlight a relief. She stopped where Elliot, aka Badger, was holding a vigil over another man, this one with similar tattoos to the ones Lucky had. Although this guy, Valeri, had them on either side of his face, down his neck and no doubt under his shirt. Blood stained the side of his jumpsuit and white shirt beneath. Ashley shifted the light, then shoved it at Badger. "Hold this." She ripped open Valeri's jumpsuit, raised the stained white T-shirt to expose more tattooed skin. Cyrillic, she thought. Intricate. Work like that took time and patience. And it hurt. A lot. She pressed her fingers against his skin. "He's got at least one broken rib. Maybe more." She couldn't be sure without X-rays.

Ashley felt Valeri's chest, abdomen, blocking out the sounds of groans and warnings continuing to come from the guard. "His pulse is weak. I'm betting he has internal bleeding. I need to get him outside. I can't work in here." She looked at the guard, whose name badge said Bradley. "I need help to move him, Bradley."

"They need your help, too." He pointed to his fellow guard and the bus driver beyond the metal grate. One look at them told her Bradley was wrong.

"They're dead. The driver has a broken neck. Your partner's chest hasn't risen or fallen since I've been here. And I'm still going to need them to move Valeri outside."

He glared at her. "I'm not giving you the keys to their cuffs."

"Have it your way." She reached up and pulled out the metal comb in her hair. She held it out to Badger. "Can you make this work?"

His eyes lit up and he bent out one of the teeth. "Oh, yeah, I can."

"You don't know what you're doing," Bradley

groaned as he shoved himself to his knees. "They're dangerous—"

"They're injured," Ashley cut him off. "That's all I care about." She heard a couple of clicks and Badger whipped the cuffs off Valeri's wrists, untangled them from the belly chain. "Do Lucky next. He can do yours. Then both of you come back here and help carry Valeri." She took Badger's place as Bradley moved closer. She leaned down to listen to Valeri's breathing.

"He going to make it?" Bradley asked.

"Can't say one way or the other just yet." But Valeri's breathing wasn't good. She could hear the wheezing even without a stethoscope. "I need my bag. I left it outside."

"My leg's sore."

"How about you try before you complain." Ashley caught Lucky and Badger talking outside the door. "Hey! You two planning a party? Bring me my bag!" She added to Bradley, "You can leave anytime."

"You've got to be the dumbest person I've ever met," Bradley muttered as he kicked himself free of the collapsed seat. "You're going to get yourself killed."

"My choice." It wasn't the first bad one she'd made.

Valeri sucked in a breath, blinked open his eyes. His skin was pale, making the ink stand out even more, and when he looked at her, his eyes were the color of polar ice. She laid a gentle hand on his barrel of a chest.

"Valeri, my name is Ashley. I'm a doctor. I'm going to help you, but I need you to stay still for right now, okay?"

"Yeah." He gave her a quick nod, then cursed. "Hurts. Can't breathe."

"You've got internal injuries. I'm going to do what I can, but you need a hospital. We'll get you there as soon as possible." Frustrated with waiting, she headed back to the door. "You find my phone?" Lucky didn't answer as he finished unlocking Badger's cuffs. "I need you to—"

"Doc!" Bradley yelled from inside. "He's coughing up blood!"

Ashley swore. "Hand me my bag." She caught it just as Lucky threw it to her. There wasn't time to move Valeri before she cleared his breathing. "I need more light. As much as you can give me. You have to keep him still. I don't have any anesthesia to give him." She grabbed Lucky's wrist and dragged him behind her. It was like pulling a boulder. "What do you eat for breakfast, rocks or something?"

"Cocoa Pebbles."

Ashley choked on a laugh. He had a sense of humor. Bonus point for him. They moved aside as Bradley half hobbled off the bus. "You can move? Great. Turn around. You're going to help."

Bradley narrowed his eyes as if thinking about arguing. Instead, he muttered, "Yeah, yeah," and hobbled back. In that flash of a moment, Ashley noticed how young he was. Midtwenties maybe? With bright, suspicious eyes and a head full of brown curls.

"C-can't breathe," Valeri wheezed when she dropped back down to his side.

"I know." She dug in her bag for a decompression needle. "This will hurt. A lot."

Valeri's eyes glistened. "Good. Means I'm alive."

A chill raced down her spine. His tone was pure evil. She chastised herself for the wild thought and focused again. She had a job to do.

"Here we go." She popped the cap off the thin-gauge needle and inserted it just above the third intercostal rib. She waited a few seconds, listening for the slight whoosh of air. She heard it, but it was weak, and a thin trickle of blood bubbled up and out of the needle. She'd been right. He was bleeding into his lung.

Despite the fact he was breathing a little easier, the effect wouldn't last long. The fluid would keep building. "Okay, step two. I've got to drain the spot, which means finding the tear." She shoved Valeri's clothing aside, slathered alcohol gel all over the wound. It wasn't the best way to sterilize, but it would have to do. "Lucky, he's going to fight me. You need to hold him still. Hands on his shoulders."

"How will you see?"

She'd stuck her penlight between her teeth and looked up at him.

"You do know how to improvise." Lucky did as he was told.

"What do you want me to do?" Bradley ducked down beside her.

"Hold the light," Ashley managed to say. And Bradley reached toward her mouth. "Not the penlight." Her voice was muffled and she jerked her head to the one on the floor pointed at them. "That one."

"Yeah, sorry. Here." He aimed the flashlight at Valeri's chest and gagged.

"Don't you puke," Ashley ordered after she spit out the penlight. "You wait until I'm done." With a scalpel she made a small incision into Valeri's side. As expected, his entire body tensed and he jerked. "Try not to move." She pressed two fingers into the opening, wincing as she felt for the tear.

"So, uh, Ashley…you do this for a living?" Bradley gasped.

"Hand her that tubing," Lucky ordered. "She's going to need it—"

"Now." Using her free hand, Ashley pushed the tubing in between her fingers, guiding it into the wound. "Come on, come on." Valeri groaned. Sweat broke out on his temple, trickled down his face. She couldn't believe he was still conscious. Most people would have passed out long ago. "Almost there. Almost—"

"Got it." Lucky aimed the light and they could see the blood flow freely out of the tube. He looked at her. "You're good."

"You have to say that," Ashley said with a small smile and wiped a hand across her forehead. Valeri's breathing eased. The wheezing lessened. "I'm all you've got."

She taped the tubing in place, then with assistance from Bradley and Lucky, wrapped Valeri's chest tight, leaving the tube open to continue to drain. "It'll hold until they can get him into surgery. Did 911 say how long they were going to be?" Where were the sirens? Even this far away from a town or city, she should have heard them by now.

"I didn't call 911," Lucky said and earned an approving nod from Valeri.

"What do you mean you didn't call? I told you to—"

"He doesn't follow your orders." Valeri's voice could have frozen lava. "He follows mine."

"It's time for you to go now, Dr. Ashley." Lucky grabbed hold of her arm and started to haul her to her feet. She twisted out of his hold.

It had taken her until this moment to process exactly the situation she was in. These were dangerous men. Criminals. Probably killers. "Yeah." She nodded, and swore she saw relief in Lucky's eyes. Snapping off her gloves, she then grabbed her needle and scalpel. "Right, I'll just get my stuff—"

She heard a gun cock and froze with her hands halfway to her bag.

"You're not going anywhere, Doc." Valeri's words were weak but clear.

She turned, slowly, and her mouth went desert dry. Valeri had a gun and he was holding it on her. "You're

not going to shoot me—I saved you. Saved your life."
Wrong. She could see it in the man's ice-blue eyes.
Dead eyes. Happy thoughts of her family, her friends,
surged through her to the point she shivered.

Instinctively, she looked to Lucky, who in turn
looked as stoic as a Roman statue.

Bradley gasped, his hand going to his empty hol-
ster. "That's my gun."

Ashley reached out, squeezed the young guard's
arm. "It's okay." Fear, cold as ice and twice as sharp,
sliced through her. She knew that look, that vacant
expression in Valeri's eyes. "No one else has to get
hurt. Everyone can—"

Valeri fired.

Ashley would have screamed if she'd had the
chance. Bradley's arm jerked in her grasp. For what
felt like a long moment she stared at him in shock.

"Bradley?" Ashley touched his chest, but it was
too late. The bullet had hit him straight in the heart.
He slumped out of her hold. Dead.

"Like you said, Doctor." Valeri pushed himself up on one arm. She swallowed the bile climbing into her throat as he again aimed the weapon
on her. "You're all we've got." He cocked the gun
again. "You can either come with us or join him.
Your choice."

Chapter 2

FBI Special Agent Slade Palmer, aka Lucky, froze as eighteen months of undercover work disappeared with the flash from the muzzle. All the lies, all the planning, all the endless days and nights he'd spent burrowing his way into Marko Valeri's good graces had skidded off the road along with the bus. Now, thanks to the good doctor who had been in the wrong place at the wrong time, the path before Slade twisted into a knot so intricate he couldn't see a route out.

He would have to do some serious scrambling if he was going to make it up the next rung in the ladder of Valeri's crime organization.

Dante Costas, Valeri's right hand and enforcer,

was dead. Clive, the best hacker in Cell Block A, was unconscious with a severe head injury. Javi, his own cellmate, had a broken arm, but was still mobile. Badger was relatively unscathed and as frenetic as ever. All wasn't lost. Not yet, anyway. Not if Slade could wrangle it all back together and get Valeri to that meeting on the Sacramento docks next week.

Valeri's older brother Edik had taken exception to Marko's conviction and imprisonment. Enough to draw the reclusive head of the family to the West Coast, where Slade would have his first—and possibly only—opportunity to shut down the criminal enterprise once and for all. More importantly, he'd finally have what he needed to find Georgiana, his missing cousin. If, and that was a big if, he could unravel the mess currently around him.

Whatever happened next, it looked as if it would happen with additional Feds on their tail for murder and now kidnapping. Given his handler hadn't responded to Slade's most recent check-ins, he couldn't be certain what was going on beyond the stone walls that had locked him away. He'd just have to do what he'd done all his life: push through and hope for the best.

He could feel the fear radiating off Dr. Ashley in waves. But she didn't waver. She barely blinked. A steel spine. Admiration swept through him. Not that his admiration was going to keep her alive. And that had just become task number one. Enough people had already lost their lives thanks to Marko

Valeri. Slade wasn't going to let him add Dr. Ashley to the list.

Her voice was strong when she spoke. "You aren't going to kill me."

Slade inwardly cringed.

Valeri grinned. The blood he'd been spitting had dried, leaving tracks down his chin as if a vampire had been interrupted during a feeding. "No?"

"You won't have to." Slade moved, pushing Ashley behind him enough that should Valeri choose to shoot, he'd take Slade down, too. And that, Slade reminded himself, would not do Valeri any good. Valeri needed him. He'd made certain of that. He'd had to in order to survive. "She'll come with us." Slade glanced over his shoulder and pinned Ashley with a look that he hoped she understood. "Won't you, Doc?"

She glared at him, her bright blue eyes sparking in the dimly lit bus. Good. Anger would keep her breathing.

"Dr. Ashley," he corrected under his breath.

"Boss. Hey, boss." Badger scampered back into the bus, a cell phone, one of the half-dozen burners Lucky had gotten a hold of before they left Folsom Prison for Pelican Bay, in his hand. "I got through to Taras. He and…" He broke off, looking from Valeri to Lucky. "What's going on?" He spotted the dead guard and lost whatever color remained in his face. "You killed him? This isn't good. Not good at all. I'm gonna be sick." He doubled over and heaved.

"Suck it up," Valeri ordered. "Doctor? You coming? Or staying?"

"She's coming." Slade grabbed her arm and squeezed. Valeri had to live. He was Slade's only hope of ever finding out what had happened to Georgiana. "Dr. Ashley is going to keep you alive, aren't you, Doctor? It is your job, isn't it?" Reminding her of that, reminding her that she had a life, and an obligation, would hopefully get her to focus on surviving rather than inadvertently igniting Valeri's ruthless temper.

"If an infection sets in, I can't stop it." Ashley lifted her chin and looked him straight in the eye. It was a warning and partly something else. Her expression struck him like an arrow to the heart. With all those blond curls and a steel-locked jaw, she was a cross between a warrior queen and a temptress. Both of whom would only be complications for him. "He needs surgery," Ashley continued. "He needs medication. Antibiotics. A hospital is his best bet."

"Not going to happen." Slade tugged her around a still-retching Badger and out into the easing night. "Javi? How's your arm? You want the doctor to set it for you?"

"It can wait." The young man eyed Ashley warily. "She coming with us?"

"Gotta keep Valeri healthy." Or at the very least breathing. Or... He eyed her car. It was too far away for her to escape without his help and if he helped, Valeri would make certain the next bullet that exited that gun ended up in Slade. For now, he had no choice. She'd have to stay with them.

No. She'd have to stay with him.

"It won't be long before they report the bus as late." Ashley hugged her arms around her waist. "Prisoner transfers report in according to a schedule. You won't get very far on foot. Especially with Valeri's injury. Let me go. Take my car. You can still have a good head start."

"We won't be on foot. What else is in your car?"

She pinched her lips tight and stared at him.

"Fine. You can show me." He stepped forward, and she jumped out ahead of him to lead the way. "Okay, then. Go. But don't even think about running away. There's nowhere you could go that we won't find you."

She looked to Javi, hope evident in her gaze, but the younger man simply stared back, resigned.

Ashley spun on her heel and walked to her car, taking the smallest steps he'd ever seen a human take.

"You've been trained. You're trying to stall for time." Slade's voice echoed around them despite him keeping his tone low. "Where do you work?"

"Folsom General. I'm head of the emergency department." The way she said it told him she'd be missed sooner than later. "Before that I worked at Chicago Medical Center. Trauma and emergency unit. So yes. I have been trained to deal with potential hostage and terrorist situations." She looked over her shoulder. "Extensively."

The first bubble of relief inside of him burst. He'd run training sessions like that himself, before he'd developed a talent for undercover work. Before he'd taken on this assignment. Correction. Before he'd demanded the assignment. Either way, Dr. Ashley would do what she'd been trained for. She'd bide her time and keep her eyes open, waiting for an opportunity to escape. That meant Slade wouldn't be able to take his eyes off her. "Just do as you're told and you won't be hurt."

"Don't lie to me, Lucky."

At her car, he stopped her before she could dive into two oversize black duffel bags in the back. "Your boss doesn't care if I live or die."

"He cares for the time being, since your training is the only thing keeping him alive. What is this?" He pointed to the bags.

"Portable defibrillator. The other bag has medications, extra supplies."

He turned and studied her in the pale light from the car. "Antibiotics?"

Ashley set her jaw.

"You almost had me fooled."

While he checked both bags, he glanced over his shoulder and saw Ashley undo her smartwatch and shove it into the pocket of her jeans. She jumped back when he hoisted the bags out of the car, then motioned for her to grab her suitcase. He slammed the trunk with his elbow. "Back to the bus."

"Why?" She jerked out the handle on her suitcase. "You have a magic wand to make it fly?"

Slade shook his head. "Are you trying to annoy me?"

"Is it working?" She batted her lashes over those baby blues of hers and sent all sorts of sparks shooting off inside of him. He took a step closer. She didn't move, simply inched her chin up more. "Try harder. I'm not shaking in my Gators."

Slade couldn't help it. He looked down at her neon pink plastic shoes. "What makes you think I won't kill you?"

She made a sound that sounded like a snort, then seemed to catch herself.

"I'm a convicted felon," he told her. "I've been given a life sentence."

"For what?"

"Murder. Three counts." By now the lie he and his handler had come up with a little over two years ago was rote and so ingrained even he'd begun to believe it. He'd spent the last eighteen months in prison with some of the most hardened criminals in the state, maybe the country. He'd done things he never thought himself capable of. Hurt people. Committed crimes. He'd made himself believe each and every sordid detail of Sawyer "Lucky" Paxton's life, because his own life had depended on it.

Now, Dr. Ashley's life depended on it, too.

"Who did you kill?"

"Doesn't matter." A lie. He didn't want it to matter. For some reason, he didn't want her to know just how dark that side of him was. "It only matters that they're dead and I killed them. Just like I'll kill you if you don't follow my instructions."

She smirked. "That might work on those guys, but it doesn't work on me."

He didn't have a response to that. No matter how fast his mind raced or how hard he thought.

"See? That. Right there." She circled a finger in front of his eyes. "I can see it. Shining, even as you try to hide it."

"See what?"

"A soul." She paused as a van pulled up near the bus. "What's that?"

He couldn't have ignored the hope in her voice if he tried. She probably thought it was a Good Samaritan stopping to lend a hand.

She moved away from him, and he saw her positioning herself to run toward the vehicle, toward what he assumed she thought was help. Slade turned as Valeri came hobbling out of the back of the bus, arms looped around Javi's and Badger's shoulders. Ashley slowed, then pivoted, but Slade caught up to her. She turned pleading, desperate eyes on him, which he forced himself to ignore. "It's too late," he said quietly. "That's our ride."

Ashley recognized the van as the one that had sped past her moments before the bus crashed. She hadn't noticed the driver's face, but given it was the only other vehicle she'd seen for miles, it had stuck in her mind.

Lucky was right. About pretty much everything. Running away would only delay them, while she'd prefer to keep breathing. If she was breathing, she'd find a way. A moment. An escape.

Bradley, on the other hand, had been wrong. Her impulsiveness and determination to help no matter what hadn't gotten her killed. Instead, he'd been the one Valeri shot as if he were nothing more than a minor distraction. She swallowed hard, forcing back the tears. When this was all over, when law enforcement had Valeri and the others in custody, she'd be the first one to testify at their trial. And she'd relish every moment of it. Then she'd deal with the emotional fallout.

"Out for a stroll in the moonlight?" the van driver asked.

"Shut up, Taras," Lucky growled before heaving her two bags at the middle-aged man. Taras grunted but caught both, and kept his dark gaze on her and Lucky. "Get in," he ordered.

It was all she could think to do in the moment.

"All the way in the back corner," Lucky told her. When she stepped up on the running board, he put a hand on her arm to steady her. His firm gentleness niggled at her senses. The passenger van closed around her as she wedged herself along the bench seat, Lucky right behind her. She tried to squeeze herself into the corner, but there was barely any room to breathe, let alone move. She lifted her feet onto the wheel housing and hugged her arms tight around herself. Her pulse hadn't stopped hammering since she'd first stopped her SUV. Now, as she turned to look behind her as they loaded her bags into the back, she found herself feeling oddly comforted by Lucky's presence.

"You forgot her purse."

Ashley jolted at the sound of a female voice, but any hope she might have had for sympathy or help vanished the second she locked eyes with the woman. She had a long face, narrow eyes and startling bleached white hair that hung down her back. She hoisted herself into the van, stood over Lucky and sorted through Ashley's purse. Tattoos banded down the length of one of her bare arms, toned arms that matched her overall fitness. She flipped open Ashley's wallet.

"Dr. Ashley McTavish." The woman rattled off her address, sorted through the rest of the contents of her wallet, and pulled out a picture of Ashley and her brother, Jack. Ashley's heart beat double time. The picture was recent, only weeks old, taken aboard Cole Delaney's boat. Longing prickled at her heart. How she loved these gatherings of people who had become good friends. Who had become…family. Panic tightened her chest. Would she ever go to one again? Would she ever see anyone, including her brother, again?

"Good-looking guy." The woman's brow furrowed. "Looks familiar. Husband?"

"Yes." The lie was automatic.

"Where's your ring?" The woman demanded even as Ashley tried to hide her hand under her thigh.

"I'm a doctor. I don't wear one."

"Olena, you're driving!" Taras leaned in and tossed the woman a set of keys. "Five minutes and we're out of here."

"I didn't realize you were sloppy," Olena said to Lucky before shoving Ashley's purse at him. "You left her cell in her car, too."

Ashley cringed. Would the GPS on her smartwatch work without it?

"I took care of it. Although I don't like cleaning up other people's messes," Olena snapped at Lucky. "So don't let it happen again."

"Yes, ma'am."

Ashley shivered at Lucky's tone and she closed her eyes. Clearly Olena had destroyed her phone. But that wasn't the thought that swam through Ashley's mind right now. It was the barely restrained ice in Lucky's voice. Why hadn't he been that cold with her? The fact that he seemed to want to keep her safe was about the only thing working in her favor at the moment. If she could manipulate that angle, drive a wedge between any of them, that could work to her benefit. "Well, you told her," Ashley muttered once Olena had left.

Lucky shifted and faced her. "Are you trying to

get yourself killed?" He had bent close, all but whispered the question in her ear. She shivered. And not from the cold night air.

Ashley pinched her lips together. She didn't know what had gotten into her. She had a high-stress job where unpredictability was the only predictable element. Why she felt compelled to test this guy time and again was beyond her. "May I have my bag?"

He reached behind him and plunked it into her lap. "What's your *husband's* name?"

Ashley's throat tightened. The way he said it, she suspected he didn't believe her. "Jack. He's a…" Telling Lucky her "husband" was a cop didn't seem like a good idea. "He's a painter."

"Watercolors or oils?"

"Houses. What does it matter—"

"Room for one more?" Badger barely had to duck to climb into the van. He threw himself into the seat in front of them, waggled thin, graying eyebrows at Ashley. "You want to trade seats, Lucky?"

"I could snap you like a twig," Lucky growled. "And I will. Back off."

Ashley swallowed hard as the anger and fear warred within her. She could barely grasp the situation she was in now, when it wasn't that long ago, she'd been safe in her car, on her way home.

"Just playin' with you, man," Badger said. "I got Lulu, remember? Just waiting for my call. She's plenty, believe me. Don't need another." Javi slid into the seat beside him.

"How's your arm, Javi?" Ashley couldn't stop herself from asking. She leaned forward only to have Lucky shove her back.

"Hurts like a bi— It hurts." Javi tried to shrug, but let out a hiss of breath that had her wishing for her medical bag.

"I have painkillers back there."

"You can fix us all up once we get to where we're going," Valeri said from the front passenger seat. He was still wheezing, but he was moving far more easily than she would have expected. Ashley watched as Taras and Olena climbed into the van and slammed the doors shut.

"Clive," Ashley whispered. "What about—"

"Clive's dead. No good to us now," Javi announced.

"Did Valeri—"

"No." Lucky told her. "It was the head injury." He pinned her with a look that told her to shut up.

She did so just as the tears she'd been keeping at bay finally burst free. She swiped at her cheeks before she was caught. She would not let them see her cry. She would not tremble or quake or cower. She would survive.

The van rumbled to life and backed up. Seconds later, they were on the move, leaving the bus, the bodies and any hope of Ashley's escape far behind.

Chapter 3

FBI Special Agent Eamon Quinn stood up from where he'd been crouched over the body of Folsom Prison guard Bradley Sherman. With the crime scene unit from the Sacramento field office just about finished, and the late-morning sun on the rise, he estimated the escapees had at least a seven-hour start.

The SUV that skidded to a halt on the other side of the crime scene tape was one he recognized. One he'd been watching for. One he'd been dreading.

"I can handle that for you, if you want." His new partner, Sarah Nelson, gestured to the newly arrived SUV. Sarah was young, eager, efficient, considerate and smart. What she was not was a chatterbox, something Eamon gave daily thanks for.

"No. That's okay, Sarah. I know them." He snapped off his gloves, stuffed them in the pocket of his dark suit and approached the two detectives he was fortunate enough to call friends. "Cole. Jack. You made good time."

"Only reason we weren't here sooner was that thing won't fly." Cole, tall, lanky and with eyes as sharp as an eagle's, scanned the scene around them. To anyone else, Detective Cole Delaney looked completely calm, but Eamon knew him well enough now to see that beneath the surface, he was paddling like mad.

"We don't know much more yet than what I told you on the phone," Eamon said to Jack McTavish before he could ask. He recognized that barely restrained panic on the detective's face. Eamon had worn it nearly every day of his thirty-three years. He knew what it was like to lose a sister and only be left with questions. He just prayed they'd find Jack's sister in time. "For some reason, the case has been flagged by higher-ups in the Bureau. No one's talking. An agent named Clay Baxter is flying in from Los Angeles as we speak. As soon as I know more, you will."

"Appreciate that." Jack pulled out his cell phone. "This might help. Ashley called my wife early this morning. She was driving back from Shasta Lake and I'm guessing was trying to stay awake. Ashley left a message since Greta didn't hear her phone."

"I hope you told Greta not to blame herself," Eamon said automatically.

"I tried. It's easy to say it. Not so easy to believe it," Jack said. "Eden's distracting her with the baby. One less thing to worry about. I'm grateful."

"Lieutenant Santos gave us the all clear to work with you," Cole said. "Whatever you need, we're at your disposal."

Eamon nodded, not surprised at their commanding officer's offer. Not that Jack McTavish would have taken no for an answer from him.

"Agent Nelson?" Eamon called his partner over. "Agent Sarah Nelson, Detectives Cole Delaney and Jack McTavish."

"McTavish?" Agent Nelson's eyebrows shot up. "As in our abducted doctor?"

"She's my sister," Jack confirmed "I've got a recording of the call. I don't know whether Ashley meant to or not, but she left the line open." He hit the play button and held out the cell on speaker.

"Hey, Greta, it's me. Just calling to check in. I'm on my way home now. I'm free for lunch tomorrow if you want to catch up and tell me all about the honeymoon. Anyway, call me when you get a chance. Bye. Holy—"

Eamon leaned closer at the sound of the crashing vehicles. It was hard to know exactly what he was hearing. Hopefully their techs could clean up the noise. The recording went on minutes after the crash ended. Muted voices, shouts. He recognized

Ashley's voice challenging someone, a very calm someone, he noted. There was a long stretch of barely audible sounds before voices grew louder again. Two voices. Ashley again and the same calm man. She told him where she worked, what was in the car. She wasn't chatty, but she'd revealed enough information to make it seem as if she was nervous. It went quiet again. Eamon was about to say something when Jack held up his finger. "Wait for it."

Eamon heard the sound of another vehicle arriving. More voices. Louder. Angrier. And another woman. "They had help waiting. Accident or not, that's not a coincidence."

"No," Cole said. "It's not. None of this is. It was a prison break."

Eamon nodded. He'd suspected as much when he spotted tire marks through the broken glass at the scene, and since they hadn't had any reports of stolen cars or abducted drivers in the area, he was leaning in that direction.

"Can you send me that recording?" Agent Nelson requested of Jack. "I can get it to our techs and see about cleaning up the rest of the conversation. Maybe someone says something that'll tell us where they're going or one of the voices will ping for recognition."

"Absolutely." While he tapped in Agent Nelson's email, Jack asked, "Do you know who was on board the bus?"

Agent Nelson glanced up at Eamon. He inclined

his head in the way he did whenever he was about to be selective about the rules. Another reason he liked working with Nelson. She had good intuition.

"If you'll excuse me, I think I hear one of the evidence techs calling for me. Detectives." She offered both Cole and Jack a quick smile before she returned to the bus.

"There was a manifest of nine including prison employees," Eamon said. "We have four prisoners unaccounted for. Dante Costas and one of the guards were killed in the crash. So was the driver." He hesitated. There wouldn't be any keeping the rest of this a secret. Not in the best of circumstances. "The other guard, Bradley Sherman, is also dead. Single gunshot to the chest. We found evidence of medical treatment in the bus. I'm guessing Ashley stopped to help."

Jack cursed and shoved his hands into his hair. "What was she thinking?"

"She's a doctor," Cole said. "She was thinking about doing her job. Same as you or I would have done. Go on, Eamon. What else?"

"The missing prisoners are Javier Selenus, Elliot Handleman, Sawyer Paxton and Marko Valeri."

"Valeri. He was just convicted of federal crimes, wasn't he?" Cole asked. "What's he doing at a state prison?"

"No idea." Eamon did his best not to sound bitter. The toxicity of bureaucratic red tape was going to be part of his epitaph. "Could be they're trying to keep him on the move so he can't regain a foothold in his organization while in prison. It's also possible he got a deal, but I wouldn't bet money on that one. That information is probably forthcoming along with Agent Baxter."

"What were they even doing on this road?" Jack looked down the road in one direction and then the other. "Transports to Pelican Bay usually take I-5 direct."

"Another good question. I'm guessing the road construction's got something to do with it, but it's on our list of things to ask," Eamon said. "Could be they were trying to keep this one quiet given who was on board."

"Clearly it wasn't quiet enough," Cole said.

Exactly what Eamon had thought. Someone somewhere had leaked the information about the transfer and the first thing on Eamon's list was to plug that hole. In just a couple of hours, he'd be meeting with the prison warden.

"Wait," Jack said. "You mentioned there were nine on the bus. Four are missing. With the dead driver and both guards, plus one prisoner also dead, that's eight. Who's left?"

"Clive Yblonski. Convicted hacker with ties to organized crime. He has a severe head injury but is still alive. Barely. He's at Folsom General. It has the closest trauma unit."

"Ashley's hospital. We should take that as a good sign," Cole told his partner. "We'll go there and wait for him to wake up, if it's okay?"

"Fine with me. I'll be able to keep my team on the search. Just don't question him without me. Call me when he wakes up. I'm going to push to keep this in the Sacramento office," Eamon explained. "If I can manage that, I'll keep you in the loop. The recording will help us get a more accurate time frame. We've got a statewide alert, although by now, they could be hundreds of miles away in any direction. Also, there's evidence at least one of the escaped prisoners was seriously injured. We're cross-checking the blood now and will know who it is soon. That's good news for you, Jack."

"What in all of this is good?" Jack frowned.

"Whoever is injured went with them. They left Clive. He's expendable. The other injured prisoner isn't. They need Ashley. And they need her alive, too." Eamon dropped a hand on Jack's shoulder and squeezed. "You hold on to that, Jack."

"Promise me you'll get her back. Eamon, promise—"

"Jack, don't," Cole said.

Eamon lifted his hand to wave off the warning. "Jack, I will do everything I can to get your sister home safe and sound." And he would.

Ashley jerked awake when the van hit a pothole the size of Cleveland. She cried out, earned quick, irritable glances from Javi and Badger before getting herself together. The crick in her neck had her slowly sitting up. Only then did she realize she'd been sleeping against Lucky's arm. She shifted farther into her corner of the van and sneaked a peek at her smart-watch. They'd been driving for nearly six hours.

She peered out the window, saw a thin line of sunlight streaming through dense trees and had no idea where they were. She'd meant to stay awake, meant to make mental notes of which routes they took. Instead, she'd lost vital information that could help her escape.

Ashley scowled and peered out the window.

"What's wrong?" Lucky asked in that hushed tone, causing her to wonder if anyone else could also hear.

"I need a bathroom."

"We're almost there," Badger told her.

"Another pothole like that and it won't matter," she muttered. "Is Valeri still alive?"

Lucky stared straight ahead. "If he wasn't, you'd know."

"Awesome." She resumed looking out the window and tried not to focus on how badly she had to use the facilities. "Anyone want to play I spy?" she asked. "I'll start. I spy with my little eye—"

Taras whipped around in his seat and aimed his gun at her. "No games. No talking."

"No fun." Sarcasm and pushing boundaries were the only things she had just then to remind herself she was still alive.

Lucky shook his head and Ashley would bet good money he'd nearly rolled his eyes. How was this even possible, Ashley wondered? How could she have been driving home one minute and found herself kidnapped with a bunch of escaped convicts the next? And one of them, the one beside her, piqued her interest entirely too much.

She almost laughed out loud, imagining her ex-husband, Adam, seeing her now. It seemed his lectures about police procedure and the undercover investigative techniques he'd honed during ten years as a narcotics detective seemed to have taken hold. Not that she was doing a great job of keeping quiet. But at least his incessant concern for her safety, combined with her training at the hospital, meant she knew how to defend herself. Or she thought she could. She winced, not wanting to take that thought very far. No doubt she was on borrowed time. As soon as Valeri was on his feet, she'd be expendable and wherever they were going, she didn't want it as her final resting place.

Adam's pursuit of undercover work, his disappearing for months on end while she was left to wonder if he was still alive, had been one of the final nails in their marriage coffin. If only she'd stayed his priority, like she had been when they were dating. The other nail had been named Bethany, who, by the time Ashley had figured things out, was already expecting Adam's baby. Seemed like an appropriate topic to dwell on, given her potential imminent death. Not.

"Wouldn't have taken you for a grinder."

Lucky's voice in her ear had her jumping again. "What?"

She looked over at Taras, who was glaring at her again. She glared back.

"You're grinding your teeth," Lucky said. "Would have thought a doctor had better ways to manage their stress."

"I missed my yoga workout this morning and a punching bag isn't available." Suddenly, her friend Allie's workout regime didn't sound so ridiculous. "Unless you're volunteering for the job?"

He just lifted a brow.

The van took a left at the fork in the dirt road and, about another hundred yards in, came to an abrupt halt.

"Okay, everyone out," Olena yelled as she pushed open the door.

A few minutes later Ashley was standing in front of a large, well-kept cabin with a strangely dilapidated shed in the back that housed a gray panel van. Other than that, she saw trees. Endless, countless trees forming a canopy over the structures that almost completely obscured the sky. And not a soul in sight.

"I'm sorry I didn't pack binoculars. I could have done a little bird-watching while I'm here," Ashley muttered.

"You do know the rest of us can hear you, right?" Badger asked her.

It was on the tip of her tongue to ask whether that

was a good or a bad thing, but once again, Lucky's hand locked around her arm and he tugged her up the porch steps, through a big, nicely furnished living room and down a narrow hall, past two smaller bedrooms, to a larger one in the back. He pushed her inside, pointed to another door. "Bathroom. Go."

"Bossy."

She thought he actually growled, but she didn't hang around long enough to be certain. She all but ran into the bathroom and slammed the door behind her.

When she was finally ready to leave the bathroom, she washed up, dried off and tried to peer out the small square window next to the sink. The beveled glass was too thick to break without bringing attention to herself, and besides… She put her palms flat against her hips and brought them up to measure against the window frame. Yeah. She wasn't going to fit. "Knew I should have gone back to the gym after Christmas." She pulled her watch out of her pocket and, after quick debate, took the small, framed image of a rainbow off the wall and hung her watch on the nail. She could only hope the charge would hold out long enough for someone to track it.

She was rehanging the picture when someone pounded on the door.

"Out!" Olena shouted.

Irritation slipped around the fear and Ashley opened the door. "What?"

"We have Valeri in his room," Olena said. "You will see to him now."

Sensing this was to be her job for the foreseeable future, Ashley followed Olena back down the hall to the other side of the cabin to another large bedroom. As with the living room, the furnishings were comfortable, practical and a bit on the pricey side. Subdued earth tones that reminded her of the Arizona desert, right down to the sunset painting on the wall above the king-size bed. Whoever's cabin this was probably wasn't going to take kindly to a bunch of uninvited guests taking up residence. "I'll need my..."

Taras arrived and dropped her bags at her feet.

"Thank you." She turned her attention to Valeri, wondering who this man was that so many were determined to keep him alive. From her main medical bag, she retrieved scissors and cut the prison jumpsuit away from the injured flesh. Valeri had his eyes closed, but his breathing was very deliberate. "No need to play possum unless you're meditating." She pulled the fabric away from the treatment she'd already administered and found everything surprisingly in place.

"The drive was not comfortable." Valeri didn't open his eyes.

"Tell me about it." She looked over her shoulder to where Taras and Olena stood. "Your bodyguards have a change of clothes for you? 'Cause these have had it."

Valeri's lips quirked. "Your sense of humor is both grating and inspiring, Dr. Ashley McTavish."

"I was at the top of all of my bedside manner classes." She also did what she could to forget this man had killed another in cold blood right in front of her.

"The cabin is well stocked with everything we need," Valeri said. "I made certain of it."

"Terrific."

Valeri flinched.

"I can give you something for the pain," Ashley offered.

He smiled. "Pain exhilarates me. I will withstand it."

"Suit yourself." As a physician, she hated to see anyone in pain. She might, however, make an exception for Valeri. "I'd like to leave the tube in for a bit longer. A few more hours at least."

"If that is what's best."

"What's best is for you to be on an operating table to fix that tear in your lung."

Now, he opened his eyes, and she recognized that same dead-eyed stare she'd seen seconds before he'd shot Bradley. "That is not possible."

"If I leave this tube in indefinitely, you're going to get an infection and die."

"Then you will take it out."

"If I take it out, your lung will fill up again. Surgery is the only—"

"Then operate."

"What?" Ashley couldn't believe what she was hearing. And yet...of course that's what he would say. "You want me to operate here? In a cabin in the middle of nowhere. I don't have what I need—"

"You will tell Badger what you need. Badger can get anything from anywhere."

Ashley's mind raced. She'd worked in enough trauma centers to be able to do it and do it well enough that he would likely survive. "I'll operate on one condition."

"I will not let you go."

"No kidding," she said more to herself, but had earned another quick smile of appreciation. "No guns on me while I'm doing it. From anyone." She looked over at Olena, who was currently caressing her pistol as if they were dating. "They're distracting and I don't trust any of you not to shoot me when I'm done. You have my word, I won't try to escape. I won't run. Not while you need treatment."

"And after?"

"How about we agree to pretend you're going to let me skip out of here with a basket of daisies singing show tunes. There. That's my deal." She wasn't entirely sure what gave her the courage to stare this man down, or to offer so blatant a challenge to his control of the situation, but what was she going to do? Cower in the bathroom during her stay? No chance. As long as she was alive, she could think. And thinking was what was going to save her. Ashley had confidence in herself. "I can operate later today after we've both gotten enough sleep."

"We are in agreement. Olena, put the gun away."

"But—"

Valeri spit out something in a language that sounded like Russian, but Olena did as she was told and shoved the pistol into the back of her jeans.

"It is the best I can do," Valeri stated.

"Good enough." And a win for her. She'd take what she could get. "I'll figure out what else I need as soon as I set Javi's arm."

Valeri's response was only to close his eyes.

Ashley collected her bags, avoided Olena's suspicious gaze and, after tending to Javi by splinting his arm and getting him a makeshift sling, she returned to the room Lucky had escorted her into before. She'd barely noticed the furnishings on her race to the bathroom. The dresser and nightstands were in the same style as those in Valeri's room. But it was the man emerging from the bathroom, stripped to the waist, a damp towel in his hands, who nearly struck her speechless. Whether he was a criminal or not, the way the man looked should be illegal.

"What are you doing in here?" she demanded of Lucky. He'd showered and changed into fresh jeans. He tossed the towel aside, tugged on a plain white T-shirt and looked as good as if he'd dressed in a tailored suit. "Waiting for my roommate."

Over her shoulder, she saw Olena and Taras looming in the doorway. Lucky moved toward her in a room that was suddenly much too small. He wasn't quick. He didn't swagger. It was more like a calculated approach one would expect from a lion stalking its prey. She couldn't stop the cry of panic from escaping her lips as she backed up, looking to Olena and Taras out of desperation. Her cry sparked something dark and dangerous in Olena's eyes as she watched Lucky approach, a spark that confirmed no help would be forthcoming and that whatever happened, Olena would find pleasure in it.

She held herself still as Lucky moved right past her. "We won't be needing an audience." He closed the door in their faces and locked it.

Ashley scanned the room, glanced toward the thick glass windows overlooking the dense forest. She looked to her bags, mind racing as she tried to think what she could use as a weapon. Needles, scalpels, in a pinch one of the bags themselves. He'd killed people and had been locked up for who knew how long. She braced herself as he passed by her again, this time to shove the curtains closed. The room darkened, then went bright again when he clicked on a bedside lamp.

Despite her wobbly legs, Ashley remained on her feet and watched every single move he made.

"They think you'll be mine. You're safe."

"Safe?" she croaked.

He inclined his head, nodded in agreement. "Safer than if you weren't. Regardless of their loitering, right now Taras and Olena are more worried about Valeri than they are you. You'd squash Badger like a spider if he tried anything and he knows it. Javi's down an arm, and besides, he's not the violent type. That leaves you one option for protection." He surprised—no, he shocked—her by walking over to the bookcase, perusing the contents as if he was in a public library. "Me."

He made it all sound so…simple. And yet nothing was simple about being locked in a bedroom with a convicted murderer.

"Where are we?"

"Knowing won't do you any good."

But knowing might keep her sane. "Where are we?"

"The last sign I saw before we turned off the highway was for Lassen National Forest."

Her mind raced, trying to remember something, anything, about their location, but as she was new to California, her frame of reference was limited.

"Asking questions is only going to get you killed, so I'd suggest you stop." He picked out a thriller, read the back cover copy, set it aside. "I'll do what I can to keep you safe, but you'll have to do your part."

"And I'm just supposed to believe that? That you'll protect me?"

"Given your other choice is to stand there in a panic, I'd say it's the better one." He didn't even bother to glance at her. "I won't hurt you, Dr. Ashley."

She wanted to believe him. More than she wanted her next breath.

"I promise. Really, you should unpack your stuff." He didn't flinch as he stood and set his chosen books on the nightstand. This time when he approached her, that initial surge of terror didn't hit in quite the same way. She straightened to her full height as he came up to her. "It's not the case with some of the others, though." His breath, warm and sweet, touched her face. "They need to believe you're mine." She forced herself to look into his eyes, eyes that seemed transfixed on her lips. On her hair. How could such a man, a man of such violence and steely determination, be so gentle? So…caring? "So, how are your acting skills, Dr. Ashley McTavish? Think you'll be able to keep up?"

Odd. He seemed determined to both terrify her and convince her he was her safe harbor in this nightmare of a storm. The dichotomy settled in her already chaotic mind. He was right. Better the devil she almost knew rather than the ones lurking on the other side of that locked door. She forced her breath out, locked her jaw. "I can pretend if you can."

"Good to hear." He returned to the bed after first picking up her bags and placing them on the dresser. "Best get your list together for what you need for the surgery and then sleep. You've got a long day ahead of you."

Chapter 4

Slade scooped up the last of the meal he'd thrown together and dropped it onto a plate. The kitchen was quiet. In fact, the entire cabin was quiet, even as it pulsed with uneasy tension, but at least he finally had some breathing room to think. His time in the bedroom with Ashley had cost him moments away from the group, although information was going to be hard to come by with Valeri out of commission.

He'd learned a lot of lessons in his years as an undercover agent, the first of which was that questions were the fast track to exposure. Since his arrival at Folsom Prison, he'd kept his head down, watched for opportunities to ingratiate himself not only to Valeri, but also to his right hand, the now-deceased Dante Costas. There was little that men like Valeri and Costas admired more than loyalty other than brute strength. Silent loyalty? Even better. The incident in the mess hall that had nearly cost Slade his eye had been his final foray into Valeri's operation. One step closer to Slade's ultimate target: Valeri's brother.

That didn't mean Slade knew everything that was going on. He sure hadn't expected a transfer to Pelican Bay along with Valeri and his crew. It was good in a way. That meant he was trusted enough to bring along on their escape. But he had questions. So many questions, but making inquiries now, with Dr. Ashley McTavish's life hanging in the balance as well, would only wreak more havoc than was already swirling. He was back to listening, learning and improvising every minute. He only wished he knew what had triggered the sudden transfer. Three days' warning seemed short notice. That it had come out of the blue told him the circumstances around Valeri's situation—possibly his conviction and imprisonment—had made someone very, very nervous.

Slade had been left scrambling to convey the information to his FBI colleagues. He could only hope they were paying as close attention to things as he was. If they didn't catch that burner phone he'd stashed on Clive…

"Princess sleeping it off?"

"This is no fairy tale, Badger." Slade feigned disinterest as he circled around the short, scrappy man who, unfortunately, could prove to be useful. "You get those supplies she asked for?" He glanced at the clock, made a mental note of how long Badger had been gone.

"Done and dusted." He scrubbed a hand through his thin, scraggly hair. "Ain't nothing I can't find. You know how many cabins are around? Dozens. And that's just on this side of the lake."

"Lake?" Slade hadn't had the chance to explore the area, but he was chomping at the bit to do just that. "You go swimming, too?"

"Ain't no one going to swim that lake in this weather." Badger scurried around him to plunder the fridge.

That was probably true. Mother Nature hadn't yet taken the full plunge into spring and continued to flirt with the chill of Jack Frost.

"You and the doctor work up an appetite, then?" Badger asked with a snicker in his voice.

Slade ignored him. He was well versed in Badger's proclivity to irritate. It was a character quirk Slade hoped to exploit in the coming days.

"Pretty snazzy digs, huh?" Badger changed the subject when he didn't get the response he was clearly hoping for. "Valeri was right. We've got some fancy surroundings while we wait out their search for us."

It didn't surprise Slade one bit that they'd ended

up at the Four Seasons of cabin getaways. Wherever Valeri went, he went in style. Even Valeri's prison cell had enough comforts to make him look as if he were sitting in the penthouse of a four-star hotel. All of that increased Slade's determination to dig deep into who else Valeri was working for.

It was his only hope of finding out what had happened to his cousin.

Keeping his head down while protecting Dr. Ashley McTavish would prove interesting. He had enough issues keeping himself alive; now he needed to do the same for her. She was a distraction. A complication. But she was also one of the bravest people he'd ever met in his life. He returned to the fridge, pulled out a couple of bottles of water, grabbed two of the rolls left on the counter.

"You gonna fix my meals, too, Lucky?" Badger guffawed and nearly fell off the stool he'd perched on.

"Don't play with the guard dog, Badger." Taras strode in, a bottle of beer joining the growing collection of empties on the side counter. "He's been known to bite. Or so I hear."

Slade merely lifted the tray and headed back for the bedroom he'd claimed for Ashley. He knew full well what his reputation was. He'd earned it. He'd worked for it. And he'd done things he never thought he was capable of to gain what little leverage he had with Valeri. He needed to get his head together. He needed to push Special Agent Slade

Palmer back down into the recesses of his mind and let convict Sawyer "Lucky" Paxton take command once more.

He stopped short before he crashed into Olena.

"Aren't you sweet." Olena offered him one of those sickly sweet smiles that never reached her vacant eyes. "Almost romantic." Her weak Ukrainian accent sounded flat, telling Slade she'd spent considerable time in the States. That voice of hers, however, was pure steel. Slade didn't know a lot about her other than she was one of the few people, along with Taras, that Valeri trusted implicitly. Which made her dangerous.

"As if you'd know what romantic is." Taras claimed another beer and twisted off the cap. "Jealous, Olena?"

"Cautious," she spit. "There is something not right about her." Olena reached behind her and pulled out an engraved dagger. She aimed it into the light, her lips curving upward as the blade glinted. "She is too perfect. Too calm. She was just there. At the crash."

"If she hadn't been, Valeri would be dead." Slade didn't like the turn Olena's thoughts were taking.

"I know." But she didn't sound convinced. "I cannot help but think that despite the crash, everything has gone far too well."

"I'd attribute that to excellent planning." Badger toasted them with a beer. "You're welcome."

"I doubt Dante would agree with you," Slade

said, well aware he was being baited. But he didn't say any more. Dante Costas's death left a big gap in Valeri's organization. One that, given the chance, Slade could walk right in to. If he didn't let distractions get in the way. "How's Valeri?"

"Sleeping." Olena glanced at the clock over the sink. "I've been told to wake him in an hour. You might want to alert your doctor."

"Well ahead of you." Slade lifted the tray and headed down the hall, stopping for a moment to hear any subsequent comments.

"Everything okay?" Javi walked out of his bedroom, his expression guarded. Not for the first time, Slade found himself wishing Javi hadn't gotten himself involved with Valeri. There was something Slade believed was still redeemable about the kid who had had his share of knocks in life, making him wonder just how deep into all this Javi was.

"Yes." Slade had earned a reputation with the crew as a man of few words. Changing now would only heighten any suspicion of him.

Javi looked toward Slade's bedroom door. For the second time since the crash, Slade caught an expression of remorse on the younger man's face. "Valeri's gonna kill her, isn't he?"

"I'm more concerned about Olena," Slade said. Another thing he'd learned early on—sowing discord could do more effective damage to the bad guys than most intricate plans of deception.

"She doesn't deserve to die," Javi said.

It was on the tip of Slade's tongue to ask if anyone deserved to die, but that was Slade talking. Not Sawyer Paxton. He'd taken one risk already, convincing Javi to tell Valeri and the others that Clive was dead. Hearing about Clive from Javi gave an authenticity they wouldn't hesitate to question. But if Slade said anything more to Javi that went against the man's survival instincts, anything else that might hint at Slade being anyone or anything other than Sawyer "Lucky" Paxton, Ashley wouldn't be the only one Valeri would kill. And then all hope of finding Georgiana would be lost.

For that reason, Slade didn't respond. He just headed down the hall to the bedroom door.

The light on the bedside table still glowed.

Fully awake now, Ashley turned her head, stifling the swirl of thoughts she couldn't reconcile. It had been hours since the accident. By now someone would have found the bus. Hopefully Greta would have checked her voicemail. She had no way of knowing how much of the accident and subsequent events had been recorded, but she was going to hope for the best and pray Jack was on the case.

If anyone could track these prisoners down, if anyone had a hope of finding her, it was her brother. The only thing she could do in the meantime was stay alive. Time and information would give her all she needed to do that.

Speaking of information, she reached for the

books Lucky had chosen for himself and flipped through the pages of one. Lucky. How had he earned that moniker, she wondered? Given his situation, not to mention his conviction record, and that angry scar that could have cost him his eye, she couldn't fathom the connection.

Just about everything about the man was a complete contradiction, but that wasn't nearly as confusing or as inappropriate as Ashley's reaction to him. How could a man like that make her feel, well, safe? Forget that. How could she be attracted to someone like him? Going by how he handled each situation as if he'd been rehearsing for it all his life told her he was a man well-versed in criminal activity and yet...

His selection of classic science fiction and biographical titles had her questioning her own prejudices about the guy.

After setting Javi's broken arm earlier, she'd found Lucky sitting quietly in the chair in the corner of the room, reading—or pretending to read—while she'd taken inventory of the medical supplies. It was as if he was more a resigned college professor needing his literary fix than a convicted murderer and kidnapper. She should have been focusing on finding a way out of here, not dwelling on Lucky's reading habits. If only she knew where here was.

Her review of the supplies had been quick. There wasn't a lot she needed, unfortunately. She was hoping there would be something that would raise a red flag wherever Badger would need to go get it, like sedatives or antibiotics. Sadly, she had enough of all of that. If she did request something and then not use it, she'd only be jeopardizing herself. Unfortunately, the items she did require could be found at any drugstore. When she'd handed off the list to Lucky, he'd offered a thank-you, shocking her, once again, into uneasy silence before he'd left, instructing her not to lock the door after him, that he'd be back in just a moment.

When he'd gone, she'd considered locking him out anyway, but trust had to go both directions. And trust could be one more weapon in her arsenal. Instead, she'd chosen to lock the bathroom door and have a shower.

He was sitting in the chair again when she emerged from the bathroom in fresh clothes and silently slipped beneath the covers. Despite lying still, she was unable to stop her mind from racing. Asleep, she was vulnerable. Asleep, she'd be in far more trouble than she was awake, and yet, soon, she couldn't keep her eyes open.

"You're safe, Ashley."

Her eyes snapped open and she looked at him, the shadows playing against him. He didn't even glance up, simply turned a page and settled back.

"Get some sleep."

"You'll stay?" She couldn't believe the question had even formed, let alone escaped her lips. Was that hope in her voice? Was she seriously asking this…this murderer not to leave her alone?

He lifted his chin, his gaze finding hers in the dimly lit room. "I'll stay."

Why that eased her mind, she couldn't explain. But she'd slept.

Now, hours later, she lay in the enormous bed, curled into a tight ball. When the door creaked open, she scrambled, curling against the headboard, and watched Lucky come into the room carrying a tray.

The laugh that escaped her lips turned into an odd cry. Hysteria, she told herself. Shock and hysteria, except there was something almost comical about this man, a man more suited to bouncing raucous patrons out of a nightclub than carrying what constituted a tea tray for an afternoon snack.

"I figured you'd be hungry by now." He set the tray beside her and backed away. "We wouldn't want you getting the shakes while you operate."

"Mustn't accidentally cut the psychopathic prisoner, right? Oh, the trouble that would cause." She flinched at the irritation that flashed across his scarred but handsome face. "I get cranky when I'm hungry." And she hadn't eaten in so long her stomach was beginning to howl. She pulled the tray closer, sat upright and stared, dumbfounded, at the plate. "What is this?"

"Some chicken-stir-fry thing from the freezer." Lucky settled again in his chair, picked up his book.

"It's probably awful compared to what you're used to eating."

"You'd be surprised what I'm used to eating." She stabbed a piece of chicken, added a clump of broccoli and ate. The tangy sauce danced on her tongue and set her stomach to growling in anticipation. "It's actually good."

"You must be starving."

She shrugged, cracked open the bottle of water, drank almost all of it.

"Is Jack a good cook?"

"Jack?" It took her a minute to remember her lie about her brother. "Oh, Jack. No, he's quite terrible. We live on takeout." That part was true enough, although her sister-in-law employed a personal assistant who was also an aspiring chef. Ashley had copped more than her fair share of meals out of their fridge.

"You need to get better at that."

"Better at what?" She took another bite, chewed until the food turned to dust in her mouth.

"Lying."

"I'm not—" She went silent at his look. "So, you have culinary skills."

"Most people can operate a microwave."

"Can't cook, then?" It was, possibly, the worst attempt at small talk in the history of small talk.

"I've been known to make a mean peanut butter sandwich."

She forked up some rice. "How normal of you."

Why did the thought of this man making a peanut butter sandwich conjure up such interesting images in her mind? "So. Has my execution time been set?"

"Don't do that."

She arched her brow.

"Make light of this situation. There's nothing light about it. Valeri may kill you as soon as you're of no use to him. Or, more likely, he'll pass along the privilege to Olena. She's begging for it."

"Is she?" Her job often required her to split her brain into two parts: the practical, trained doctor who was ready for anything and the homebody, closet knitter who, until recently, had been debating getting a cat. More times than not she was grateful for the duality. Take now, for instance, when she could turn on the emergency room doctor like a switch and block out the horrific thought of her life ending in the near future. "Why, I wonder?"

"Why?"

"Why does she want to do that? Don't you ever think about it?"

"Think about what?" He looked truly baffled, his eyes narrowing, his brow furrowing. His twisted-up expression accentuated the scar that reached from his temple to his cheek.

"Think about why people are the way they are. She's dead inside. One look in her eyes and you see that. She's ice. Even more than Valeri, and I'm guessing he's pretty cold."

Lucky inclined his head as if examining a very confusing puzzle.

"What's Valeri done? No, wait. Never mind." She shook her head and returned to eating, even though she was far beyond being able to taste anything. "I don't want to know about who I'll be saving."

"Will you save him?"

His question surprised her. "Don't you want me to?"

"Not particularly. But I need you to."

There it was again. That duality of his. That they felt the same way, that their personalities were similar, struck her as strange, almost funny. Just when she thought she'd figured him out, he went and said something that shifted her expectations yet again.

"He won't let you leave this place alive."

She swallowed hard, looked back down at her plate. "I know."

"And you'd still save him. Knowing that?" He leaned forward in his chair, arms resting on his knees.

"Yes. I took an oath. Just because the patient is reprehensible and likely irredeemable doesn't lessen my promise or obligation."

"So everyone is worthy of saving. Is that what you're saying?"

Why did she suddenly feel as if she was back in her college philosophy class again? "What I'm saying is my oath as a doctor is to help when I can and not to do any harm. The rest is out of my hands."

"You're naive, Dr. Ashley McTavish." He rose quickly when the doorknob suddenly rattled. He walked over and punched a fist into the pillow beside her, rumpled the sheets and, as she watched, dumbfounded, stripped off his T-shirt and threw it on the floor.

She couldn't move. Didn't dare move as he headed to the door, unbuttoned his jeans and braced his arm on the frame. It was only then that he pulled open the door. "What?"

"We're setting up for Valeri." Olena's voice drifted into the room.

Ashley sank back against the headboard, trying to stay out of view.

"She needs to get ready. Now."

Ashley jumped at the sound of Olena's hand slapping hard against the door. Lucky tightened his grip, kept it from opening wider.

"We're busy."

The tone in Lucky's voice shocked Ashley to the marrow of her bones. Jekyll and Hyde. Only… which was which? And could she honestly trust either of them?

"Make it quick, then," Olena ordered. "The sooner we're rid of her, the better."

For the second time, Lucky slammed the door in Olena's face.

She was suddenly so cold. Cold and shivering and…her stomach churned. Without another word, she bolted out of the bed and into the bathroom, barely making it to the toilet before she vomited up the meal he'd prepared for her.

A cold sweat broke out on her face, coated her skin. Gentle hands brushed at her shoulders and scooped her hair away from her face. Her body trembled but his calm presence behind her helped. She sank back on her heels, shuddering. She heard the water running in the sink, but didn't have the energy—or perhaps it was the courage—to open her eyes. The next thing she knew, she felt a cool, damp cloth pressed against her forehead. "She is going to kill me," she whispered. It was as if she'd come out of a fog and walked straight into her reality. "You can't stop her forever." She'd heard the promise, the excitement, in Olena's voice. "If Valeri dies—"

"You aren't going to let him die, remember?" Lucky stated. "That's your first job. Keep him alive."

"My first? What's my second?" She finally opened her eyes.

His hesitation nearly made her scream. "Trust me."

"Trust you. Trust *you*?" She already had, to a point, but that was before she'd let the reality of her situation sink in. She was surrounded by convicted felons who hadn't batted an eye at killing a prison guard. Who had walked over Dante's body as if he were nothing more than a sack of sand. "Who are you that I should do that? What are you?"

"What matters is I take promises as seriously as you do. Do you believe that?" His eyes remained steady on hers. He didn't blink. Didn't flinch. Just stared.

"I suppose."

"Don't suppose. Believe it. I will get you out of here, Ashley. I will get you home to Jack. I'll find a way. But first, I need you to make sure Valeri is going to live. Can you do that?"

She nodded. "That's the easy part."

"Good. Then get cleaned up. You've got an operation to perform."

That she hadn't had a panic attack sooner was a minor miracle, Slade thought. Even for someone as well trained as Dr. Ashley McTavish, there had to come a point when circumstances showed her how bleak her situation truly was. Thankfully that moment had happened out of sight of anyone other than him—the one person who was willing to push her through to the other side.

He'd made a promise. Another promise that could cost him everything. But he'd find a way—any way—to get her back to her family.

Valeri might be many things but forgiving was not one of them. Despite her usefulness, she was a complication that threatened his future and plans for escape and reinvention.

"I need more light." Ashley's voice was muffled behind the tight breathing mask. Javi and Taras had moved Valeri into the sun porch, where a makeshift surgical center had been created by hoisting a picnic table from outside onto cinder blocks. They'd scrubbed the table clean, obviously, and covered it in multiple layers of sheeting, draping plastic tarps on the floor and bringing in every lamp they could find in the expansive house. "Here." Ashley pointed a finger toward the wound she'd clamped open with one of the only two clamps she'd had in her bags.

Slade had watched, taking a mental inventory as she'd unloaded her supplies. Some agents went undercover with an ace up their sleeves. A contingency plan only they knew about in case something went seriously wrong. Slade was one of those agents, but the plan would have been more easily executed had Clive Yblonski not gotten knocked sideways and scrambled his brain in the bus crash. He'd been Slade's intended cover if he needed a fast exit. The guy was a communications expert, could rig a cell phone to call the International Space Station, but as for strategizing and deception, he wasn't the brightest. "Lucky, here, please." Ashley's voice cut through his reverie and he did as he was told, reangling one of the lamps toward the opening in Valeri's chest. "What's his pulse?"

Olena kept her fingers on Valeri's wrist. "Steady. No change."

"Good. Let me know if there is."

Slade had to give Ashley serious credit. It was like a switch had been flipped inside her, turning off the fear that had her sick in the bathroom and turning on the controlled, no-nonsense physician.

That she'd asked Olena to monitor Valeri's pulse surprised him, but then he realized it was because it was the one way Ashley could be sure to keep Olena in sight. Multitasking at its best.

"There it is." She angled the clamp down and peered closer. "The tear isn't as large as I thought. That's the good news." She winced, ducked down a bit.

"What's the bad?" Taras asked from the doorway.

"Put on a mask," Ashley snapped.

Badger scrambled forward and pushed one into Taras's hand. Slade looked beyond Valeri's protector and saw Javi standing behind him looking slightly ill.

"What's the bad news?" Slade asked.

"It's going to be a pain to stitch." She reached for a stack of gauze and pressed it into the opening. She blew out a breath. Sweat dotted her brow and she blinked, widened her eyes as if trying to focus. "Badger, come here. I need your small hands."

Taras snorted. Badger glared at him but did as she asked, coming to her side, gloved hands outstretched.

"I need you to hold this gauze in place, dab at any blood you see popping up, okay? Here." She handed him more gauze. "I want to get Valeri stitched up and closed fast. The risk for infection is already way higher than I'd like."

"Would a can of spray disinfectant help?" Olena asked in that simpering tone of hers.

"A hospital would help. Okay, here we go." With the surgical thread and needle she'd prepared earlier, she got to work, drawing the raw edges of Valeri's lung together. "There, Badger. Can you get that? Yeah. Good. Great. Thanks."

Watching her work, watching her literally stitch a man's body back together, left Slade nearly speechless. What doctors, what people like Ashley McTavish did far surpassed any ability he possessed to make a difference, something he'd wanted to do from before he'd even earned his badge. Bad timing aside, he'd never felt so inferior in his life. Or so utterly transfixed and impressed.

"All right. One down. Two to go." Ashley gently instructed Badger on how to extract the gauze, then had him backing away as she stitched up the surgical cut and where the tube had been inserted. By the time she stepped back and snapped off her gloves, she looked exhausted. But that spark of defiance in her eyes went straight to Olena. "Pulse steady?"

"Yes."

"Good. The propofol should wear off in a few hours. Let's get him back into his room. Take the entire table," she ordered when Taras and Javi entered. "Try not to jostle him." Ashley ripped off her mask and gathered up her clamps and surgical instruments. Olena got to her feet as Valeri was taken out, moving to block Ashley. "What?"

"Where are you going with those?"

"To the kitchen. I need to wash and try to sterilize them."

"No."

Slade grimaced. Why was it every plan he came up with these days seemed to be at the mercy of Ashley McTavish?

"Get out of my way," Ashley told her.

Badger scampered off, dropping his gloves onto the plastic tarp under their feet.

"I don't trust you," Olena stated, her hand going behind her back.

"The feeling's mutual," Ashley snapped. "Look, I just stitched up your boss and until he's conscious again, you still need me. So, if you'll excuse me, I'd like to spend my last few minutes of life scrubbing his blood off my hands." She shoved passed Olena so hard and so fast, Slade found himself blinking in shock.

"I cannot wait to end her. Arrogant, idiotic…"

"She's a doctor," Badger chimed in, casting a glance at Ashley. "What if one of us also gets hurt? I vote we keep her."

"She's not yours, Olena." Slade made certain his tone caught every bit of Olena's attention. She turned and faced him, then smiled as if daring him to say more. So he did. "You want to get to her, you'll need to go through me."

"Now that's a challenge I'd enjoy. Go watch your doctor, Lucky. And pray your name holds out."

Chapter 5

FBI Special Agents Eamon Quinn and Sarah Nelson exited the fourth floor of Folsom General Hospital about the time the last of the caffeine left Eamon's system. Though the scene of the bus crash had been processed and cleared, they were still waiting for lab results along with the updated files on the escaped prisoners.

Eamon's meeting with the warden hadn't provided much information beyond what they already knew. The prisoner transfer request had come through official channels. The only odd thing was that Javier Selenus's name had been added to the list of transfers at the last minute. The prisoners' abandoned belongings were currently stashed in the back of Eamon's

SUV. When Eamon had pushed for details about the route and timing of the transfer, the warden had stated that must have been at the driver's discretion as he had no knowledge of any changes.

Eamon was back to waiting for answers from SA Clay Baxter.

The day felt like a complete waste, given everywhere Eamon turned it was as if he was being blocked. Even his direct supervisor hadn't returned his calls, which told Eamon two things. First, this was more than just a typical prison break. And second, Ashley McTavish was in even greater danger than he'd initially believed.

He was not looking forward to imparting either tidbit of information to her detective brother, Jack.

The day, like so many others, felt like a week. Right now, he was desperate for a shower, a burger and a coffee the size of Lake Tahoe, but he wanted to lock this case down before he surrendered to creature comforts. Getting Ashley home to her family and friends was his number-one goal.

"Clive Yblonski's room, please." Sarah flashed her badge at the nurses' station. A young nurse looked up.

"Are you the agents working on Ashley's case?" An older woman with short-cropped gray hair, wearing scrubs with hot-air balloons on them, put a calming hand on the younger nurse's shoulder.

"Yes, ma'am." Sarah nodded.

"Follow me, please. I'm Patricia Calhoun. I

work with Ashley sometimes in the emergency room." Her thick-soled shoes squeaked along the gray-speckled linoleum. "We're all just stunned by what's happened. It's surreal. Is there any more news yet?"

"No, ma'am." Eamon kept his voice neutral.

"Well, I suppose even if there was, you couldn't tell me. We all love Ashley. She's an amazing doctor, obviously, but she's also a really nice person, you know?"

"Yes, ma'am," Eamon repeated. He knew full well how nice Ashley was. He'd met her on a few occasions and found her to be charming, clever with a quip and smart. He was glad at least two of those qualities would work in her favor with her kidnappers.

"Dr. Price is on vacation. He's in charge of the neurology department, but I called him to see if it would be all right if we got you set up in one of the meeting rooms until this situation is resolved. I can get you a bigger space if you need it, but this is closest to Mr. Yblonski. I know time is important here."

"Ma'am?" Sarah frowned, clearly as confused as Eamon felt.

"I'm sorry. Jack's made it clear he isn't leaving until either Ashley's found or Mr. Yblonski regains consciousness. I'd lay odds on the former happening sooner than the latter." She stopped beside a room with glass walls and gestured to the figure lying unconscious on the bed inside. The monitors beeped their familiar, steady rhythm. "Mr. Yblonski suffered significant brain trauma. There's swelling, so they've put him into a medically induced coma."

"For how long?" Some of the hope that had bolstered Eamon throughout the day faded. They needed information and Clive was the closest thing they had to a witness.

"It could be hours, could be weeks. Until the swelling goes down, this is how he'll be." Nurse Calhoun glanced at the two police officers standing on either side of the door. "Cole insisted on the guards. He suggested they might be needed."

"He's right," Eamon agreed. Anyone remotely connected to Marko Valeri, both in and out of prison, was being questioned. He didn't think a coma would prevent anyone from thinking Valeri's computer genius was a threat. "I hope having the guards around won't be too much trouble." He recognized both uniformed officers from Cole and Jack's squad at Major Crimes in Sacramento and reminded him how close-knit the unit—and their extended families—were.

"In their own way they're helping to find Ashley," Nurse Calhoun said and continued down the hall. "They aren't any trouble at all." She moved aside to let Eamon and Sarah slip into the meeting room. "Oh, Jack, I was just bringing the agents to you."

"Thanks, Patty. Any word?" Jack's snappy tone told Eamon he was getting as frustrated as Eamon was. They both had enough experience to know the longer a kidnapping went on, the lower the odds were that they'd see Ashley safe again.

"Let's talk inside," Eamon said. "Thank you, Ms. Calhoun." He stepped inside the meeting room. "Tell me there's coffee," he pleaded with his friends.

"Way ahead of you," Cole called out to him. The space had definitely been usurped by the team, right down to the sea of laptops and connected cables, and a magnetic whiteboard covered with pictures and notes scribbled in black ink. But it was the stack of takeout boxes on one of the tables that had him pining. "Greta asked Vince to bring us dinner. Vince, you remember Eamon Quinn from the FBI?"

"Sure." Vince offered his hand. "Glad to see you're on this."

Eamon returned the handshake. Vince Sutton, bar owner, former Marine and husband of District Attorney Simone Armstrong-Sutton, had a wide and varied past, not the least of which was as one of the best private investigators in Northern California. He and his brother, Jason, along with Max Kellan, a former firefighter, had earned stellar reputations in recent months because of their work with law enforcement and by assisting Cole's wife, Eden, to solve cold cases.

"Unfortunately, the burgers are probably cold by now, but help yourself," Vince told them.

"They could be ice cubes and I'd eat one." Sarah

grabbed two boxes and handed one to Eamon. "Thanks."

"Least I could do." Vince motioned them over to the main table, where Cole was tapping away on a laptop. "So we're finalizing a search grid radius. Folsom and Sac Sheriff's Department are stream-lining it now."

"We've got a search grid already," Sarah mum-bled around a full mouth as Eamon stuck a pod in the coffee maker and brewed a cup.

"We know," Cole said. "But it's a lot of ground to cover so we're trying to close in on where they are eventually headed."

"Meaning they never expected to reach Pelican Bay." Eamon had to admit, he'd already come to that conclusion.

"That's our guess," Vince chimed in and waved them over. "The bus crashed on a back road off Highway 70. Even if they detoured off I-5 to avoid the construction, that's an out-of-the-way route to take. It would have been a deliberate choice. That tells me that pretty much from the time they left Folsom, they'd already planned the detour."

"Those buses are equipped with GPS. They're tracked the whole time." Sarah gulped and reached for a water. "Unless…"

"Unless someone hacked into that system and the driver was in on the escape? Yeah. Way ahead of you." Vince handed over a file. "Jason ran a deeper background check on the driver, Monty Williams.

Hired just three months ago and before that, he worked for a private security firm in Los Angeles. That's where his trail ends." He flipped open the file to a blank page. "Zip. Nada. Up until ten years ago, the guy doesn't exist. Most employers don't go back further than a decade, anyway. So he's invisible. And this was his first solo bus run. Every one before, he's had a supervisor running shotgun with him. But not yesterday."

"Lab has the GPS from the bus," Sarah said. "They'll be able to confirm if the system was hacked."

"What security firm was Williams with?" Eamon had his phone out and was already typing.

"ClearMont," Cole said. "No use looking for it. It closed up a little over three years ago. No trace of any of the owners or their employees. Even internet details are sketchy, which meant their presence there at the time was negligible. Probably a shell company."

"That's good work." Sarah looked over at Eamon, who had the strange feeling Cole and Jack were holding something back from them. "How did Agent Baxter and his team not come up with that?" she asked.

"Good question." One of about a hundred Eamon had racing around his head. His phone chimed with an incoming text that he quickly read. "One we might finally get an answer to. SA Baxter's on his way up. He's put any and all information on lockdown where Marko Valeri's concerned. No one's talking. Said he'll explain when he gets here."

"About time," Jack muttered as Eamon retrieved his coffee. "He was coming from LA, not the Antarctic. Yblonski hasn't been any help."

"Maybe not." Sarah pulled out her cell and scanned the screen. "But this might be. Tests confirm the blood type we found in the bus matches Marko Valeri's. Only Valeri's, given the other prisoners' health records. With the amount of blood at the scene, Forensics are saying he's probably not in great condition. Hang on. I've got a call coming in." She went outside to take the call.

"He'll be okay if Ashley's taking care of him," Jack said. "Is that good news or bad? I'm not sure."

"Unknown. What *else* did you find out?" Eamon asked. Jack and Cole simply stared at him. "Guys, come on. We're working together, remember? What are you holding back?"

Vince frowned and pulled out his wallet. "Should have realized you two would know Eamon that well." He handed over a twenty to Cole, then pulled open a cabinet and grabbed a large clear plastic bag with an orange jumpsuit and other clothing items inside. "Nurses gave us everything that was on Yblonski." He tossed it and a second, smaller baggie on the table. "Yblonski had a cell phone on him. A burner, no doubt. We were going to have it analyzed ourselves."

Eamon looked down at the phone. "I'm guessing

you assumed that once you gave that to me, whatever information there is on the phone wouldn't be shared with you all."

"Sounds about right," Cole admitted.

"You were okay with holding back evidence in a federal crime case, and sending it to your own lab for analysis?"

"We didn't say we were going to send it to our lab," Jack said. "But if it would lead us to Ashley, you bet I was."

Eamon stared at the clear plastic bags. He knew exactly what Jack was feeling: helpless, angry. Defiant. Combined, they were a recipe for career destruction and should Jack have made the wrong choice... Jack was on the edge of doing so now. So was Eamon.

"Thank you for turning over this evidence." He pulled the larger bag toward him and set it aside, leaving the cell phone on the table. "The FBI appreciates your cooperation." The door snapped open. Eamon looked over his shoulder and when he glanced back at the table, the phone was gone.

"That him?" Jack walked over to the door as Sarah returned to them, followed by another man. "He always travel with an entourage?"

Eamon joined him, a bit surprised at the two other agents trailing behind Special Agent Baxter. "He's got a reputation as a bit of a rock star," he murmured to Jack. "His closure rate is off the charts. He's cool, rational. Dedicated. Chooses only the best of the best for his team. And he's by the book right down to his regulation socks."

"You guys have regulation socks?" Cole asked Sarah, who tugged up the hem of her pants to show off bright bumblebees with light sabers.

"Don't know if they're Bureau regulation," she said with a grin and reached for the rest of her burger. "But they work for me."

"Agent Baxter's a closer, Jack." Eamon shifted his attention back to the approaching agents. "He doesn't like to give anything away and only trusts those closest to him." And that circle was pretty small. "Whatever he knows, we need to know, so play nice."

"I always play nice," Jack scoffed.

Eamon considered that for a moment. He supposed that was true. But he also knew playing nice often got thrown out the window when family love and loyalty were involved.

"Agent Eamon Quinn. SA Clay Baxter." Wire-rimmed glasses magnified pale blue eyes. Baxter's dark hair was dotted with specks of gray, the strain around his eyes evidence of a long day. The soft-sided briefcase in his hand looked as if it weighed a ton. "We need to speak privately."

"With all due respect." Eamon shifted slightly to the side to block Jack from pouncing. "I've worked with Detectives Delaney and McTavish in the past and it's Detective McTavish's sister who's been kid-napped. Whatever you tell me is going to be conveyed to them, so let's save time." He stepped back and waved him forward. "Please."

Baxter looked less than thrilled, but he did as requested. Eamon closed the meeting room door. The other two agents all but rode Baxter's coattails as they moved to flank him. Neither agent was familiar to him, but both were about the same age, midthirties, and had a similar steely-eyed look and a dark suit. All that was missing were the trademark shades.

"Agents Flynn and Robeson." Agent Baxter made quick work of the introductions. "Before we go any further, I want it made clear, the Valeri case is mine, so—"

"We don't care about your record of closing cases." Jack moved to stand between his partner and Vince. The three of them looked formidable. "All we want is my sister back. Alive. Now tell us what you know."

Eamon caught an uneasy look between Flynn and Robeson.

Baxter's eyes sharpened and he pulled himself up to his full height, which, unfortunately for him, was still a good four inches shorter than Eamon. "Marko Valeri's serving—"

"Clarification. Tell us what you know that we couldn't have found out thanks to an online search." Jack tossed a stack of papers on the table. "You've had him in custody for more than a year and yet he's still in a state facility. Conclusion? His case is still considered active, meaning the investigation into Valeri didn't end with his conviction."

Baxter's jaw tensed. "Valeri's faction is one spoke in a wheel of corruption. A wheel that's driven by his brother Edik. We attempted on multiple occasions to cut a deal with Marko, but he didn't bite. Within weeks of his incarceration at Folsom, we got wind he'd retaken control of his organization thanks to various talents he found among fellow inmates."

"Like Yblonski," Eamon said.

"Guy's nickname is Fingers. He's done some nasty stuff on the dark web." Baxter checked his watch.

"Exactly what breeze blew that information your way?" Vince asked.

"A prison informant," Baxter replied.

"Always a reliable source of information," Cole muttered.

"He was until he was found dead in his cell twenty-four hours ago," Flynn, the taller of the two agents spoke up. "It was my idea to use him to spy on Valeri. I told him we'd protect him," Flynn added and earned a glare of irritation from his boss.

There was no mistaking the bitterness in the agent's voice.

"What the kid gave us panned out," Baxter said. "Because of him, we were able to monitor most of Valeri's communications. We know of at least four prison guards on Valeri's payroll, one of which was on the bus. We've had eyes on them along with Williams, the driver. The evidence against them is solid, so when the time comes, they're done."

"Williams is already done," Vince reminded the lead agent. "He's dead."

"Right. So that thread is cut." As if Williams was no more than a bug on a windshield, Baxter continued. "We've been monitoring how the plan has been playing out. Who's signed what paperwork, who is depositing significant and unusual amounts of cash into their bank accounts. This was systematic, deliberate and well-thought-out. This wasn't just about getting Valeri out of prison. It's about him connecting with his main contact here in the States who is going to get him out of the country."

"To go where? Canada? That's twice as far as Mexico," Vince said.

"In the conversations we've overheard, there's been a lot of chatter about boats and waterways," Baxter said.

"That would mean they're heading into Sacramento rather than going farther north," Cole said. "Northern California's ripe for human trafficking routes, which is the center of Edik's business. Makes sense they'd try to get Valeri out of the country that way."

"Or get someone in unnoticed," Flynn said. "Someone like Edik."

"Edik Valeri is coming here?" Eamon asked. "He's crawling out of the hole he's been hiding in?"

Baxter nodded. "Rumor is Edik is not happy about his brother's conviction. He plans to get him a new life somewhere. Maybe South America, maybe Mexico, who knows? At least, that's the assumption."

"Assumption?" Jack's voice echoed Eamon's disbelief. "These guys have my sister! Set your assumptions aside and give us some solid facts."

"What about the other guards you know are working for Valeri? Have they been questioned?" Cole asked.

"No. They're more useful to us where they are, not stuck in an interrogation room. Or they were," Baxter said. "Your visit to the prison today, Agent Quinn, spooked one of them. He went home sick, packed up and, with his wife, headed out."

"Maybe if I'd been let in on the situation, I would have postponed my visit," Eamon said. "Or maybe my doing my job showed it was business as usual, whereas my not going would have tipped off the other two guards that they were under suspicion."

"Hard to know for sure either way," Robeson said.

"Hold on," Vince said. "You've got known corrupt officers working in a state prison, a prison that just lost five high-profile convicts, and your idea is to let them be?"

"The longer they think they're in the clear, the better the chance they'll be given more information down the line." Baxter said this as if it made complete sense.

"And what if they know about the rest of the plan? What if they know where—" Jack started, but Vince raised his hand and cut him off.

"You said you have eyes on them." Vince narrowed his gaze at Baxter. "That implies you have a contact."

Baxter didn't respond.

"You've got someone on the inside," Eamon said. The long delay in Baxter arriving. The stonewalling from the higher-ups. Suddenly it all made sense. They weren't just protecting a case. "You've got someone else feeding you intel. Someone who's with them now. No wonder no one would answer my questions when I called in. You're protecting an asset."

"Another criminal informant?" Cole asked. "A jailhouse snitch?"

"I'm not protecting a criminal," Baxter snapped, looking offended. He took a deep breath, glanced around the room as if debating how much more to say. "I'm protecting my agent."

"Your…agent?" Cole asked. "You have an FBI agent undercover as a convict in Folsom? For how long?"

The fire in Baxter's eyes had Eamon sweating. "Eighteen months."

"Eighteen months?" Vince looked more shocked than Eamon had ever seen. "What is wrong with you? Do you not know how damaging that is? How dangerous?"

"He knew the risks." Baxter moved to the table, set his case down and, after shuffling through the files, withdrew one. He opened it, turned it around to show the photo of the man that, until now, Eamon and the rest of them knew previously as Sawyer Paxton. "He wanted this case. For reasons I'm not comfortable sharing at this time."

"Special Agent Slade Palmer," Robeson said. "He's been with the Bureau for going on ten years. He's also former military. He's been one of our main training agents for security assignments. Or he was until he became one of the agency's best undercover operatives. We got him in place with the express intent of getting close to Marko Valeri. And therefore, close to Edik."

"That's—" Jack dropped into the chair nearest him. "You could have told us this hours ago!"

"No," Baxter said. "I couldn't. I couldn't tell anyone." He glanced at his team as if looking for help.

"We lost contact with Agent Palmer over a month ago," Flynn told them. "He's missed the last four check-ins. Valeri's known for keeping a close watch on all his people. He even teams them up so they watch each other. It could be as simple as Slade couldn't make the call without raising suspicion."

"What about his backup?" Eamon asked. "Who is his contact inside the prison?"

"He doesn't have one." Baxter's cool-eyed gaze remained steady.

Silence flooded the room.

"You sent your agent in there alone, without any help for more than a year." Vince let loose a string of curses that impressed even Eamon's experienced ears. "Without any escape plan?"

"We have a plan in place. This was his call," Baxter said. "I didn't question it."

"Of course not. What's one agent's life compared to your success rate?" Jack threw a hand up and sent papers flying. "What a clown show." He stalked over to the whiteboard and stared at the photos pinned there.

"Jack, enough," Eamon said, even though he agreed with his friend. He would never have sent an agent into this kind of situation without an escape, or at the very least someone to contact should the mission go bad. "Have you heard from Palmer since the crash?"

"No." Robeson looked embarrassed. "There hasn't been a call to any of the numbers we have set up for him. He's been completely silent for more than four weeks. He had one burner phone, but that number's been quiet, too. We didn't find him in the bus. So his cover probably hasn't been blown. That's a good sign."

"Is it?" Cole asked. "Is it really?"

"There's another possibility we haven't wanted to consider," Flynn said.

"Agent Flynn," Baxter interrupted.

"No one wants to voice it, and I get it," Flynn said. "I like Slade. He's a good guy and he has good reason for wanting to take Valeri and Edik down—"

Baxter swung on his agent. "He hasn't turned. I might not know everything that's going on, but I will stake my reputation on Slade Palmer's dedication not only to this case, but to the Bureau."

"Better agents than Slade have switched sides," Robeson said. "We haven't heard a word from him in weeks. Logic dictates we should consider it."

"Then let's get to the office and start digging," Flynn said emphatically and headed out. Robeson followed.

Baxter walked to the open door. "Coming, Agents Quinn and Nelson?"

"Yes, sir." Sarah moved past Eamon, a puzzled expression on her face. Eamon gave her a quick shake of his head.

"In a moment," Eamon answered and made a show of gathering up the files Baxter had left behind. When he was sure the others were out of earshot, he looked at his friends. "You get working on that phone. And in the meantime, check out Agent Slade Palmer. We need to know for certain if he's friend or foe."

Ashley sat in the dark bedroom, staring out at the equally black night. The night that was pressing in on her like a weighted blanket.

Valeri had regained consciousness a few hours before, had answered all her questions well enough to prove he was on the mend. After he drank some water, he fell back asleep. As far as patients went, he was one of the easiest she'd had in ages.

Her stomach was not happy with her after she'd forced herself to eat what some company laughingly called a protein bar. She'd found a box of them in the kitchen when she'd been cleaning her instruments. She'd stuck another two in her pockets, nearly leaping out of her skin when Taras appeared behind her and removed all her surgical tools from her sight. He'd counted them first, telling her he'd been paying attention and confirming she'd been smart not to pocket the scalpel, even though she had considered it. Being caught arming herself would have only caused problems. And she had more than enough of those already.

She dragged the blanket from the bed tighter around her shoulders, curled into the chair Lucky had claimed as his own earlier in the day.

When the door opened, she glanced over, secure in the knowledge it would be Lucky, but so tired of the way her heart leaped every time she turned around. He walked over, handed her a bottle of water. "Drink. You look pale."

"Don't tell me. You have night vision." Recognizing the effects of dehydration, she did as he suggested.

"Stress kills," he said as if she, as a doctor, didn't know that.

"So does being locked up with a group of escaped convicts." She closed her eyes, leaned her head back. "You haven't slept at all since the bus crashed."

"I don't sleep. Much." He walked over to the window. "What do you see out there?"

Freedom, she thought. Peace. *Escape.* "Fresh air."

"Is that what's causing your migraine?"

"How did you know I get migraines?"

"It's in your eyes. My cousin used to get them. Change in the weather, stress, altitude, pollen. She could blink the wrong way and get one." He motioned to the water bottle. "Dehydration."

"Aside from sticking my nose in a face full of flowers, I'd say you hit three for four."

"You should eat—"

"Stop telling me what I should do. I'm a doctor. I know what I should do." She should take the medication she had in her bag, but the pills always knocked her for a loop and right now, she didn't want to close her eyes for a second, let alone for hours.

The silence stretched razor-thin.

"Let's go." He pushed off the wall and headed to the door.

"Go where?" She eyed him, wondering what devious plan waited for her on the other side of the door.

"Outside. There's a lake not far from here. Solar lights on the path. A walk will do you some good."

"Like they're going to let you take me outside these walls."

"Do I look like a man who asks permission?"

No, actually, he didn't. Which only confused her further when she considered how kind and gentle he'd been toward her.

As grateful as she was that his protective instincts had kicked in where she was concerned, she had to admit, her situation would be a little easier if he wasn't watching her every minute. "Let me get my shoes and a sweatshirt." She retrieved both from her suitcase and laced her sneakers tight.

The sound of explosions and car crashes sounded from the living room, where Javi and Badger were battling it out on some video game. The room was littered with food remnants and empty beer bottles. Lucky took hold of her arm and led her to the front door. When he opened it, she braced herself to run.

"Where do you think you're going?" Olena exited the kitchen, a knife in one hand, a sliced apple in the other. She eyed Ashley as if she were a particularly juicy morsel.

"Out for a walk," Lucky said. "She needs fresh air."

"Another moonlight stroll?" Badger called. "How romantic!"

"She doesn't *need* anything," Olena said as Ashley's heart banged against her ribs. "She stays here."

"Contrary to your delusions of power, Valeri's

the boss." Lucky loomed over her and reminded Ashley, once again, how imposing a figure he could be. "Not you. We're going outside."

"Not alone."

"We don't need a chaperone. We'll be back in a bit." He flipped on the front-porch light and maneuvered Ashley out the door. Olena was still standing there, staring out the side window, munching on that stupid apple.

The cold hit her first, but Ashley welcomed it even as she zipped up her sweatshirt. "I don't need assistance walking." She tried to tug her arm free of his hold, but to no effect. "Lucky—"

"Sawyer. My name is Sawyer."

"Oh. All right." Why was he telling her this? The more information she had, the worse it would be for all of them should she escape. "Where did Lucky come from?"

He touched a hand to the scar on his face. "Let's just say the nickname is ironic." The cobblestones came to an end at the side of the house. The road extended and narrowed into the trees, with a well-worn path winding out of sight. He let go of her arm, but stayed close. Too close. "You aren't scared of the dark, are you?"

"I'm not scared of anything," she lied, and took the lead. She had hoped, but hadn't counted on him suggesting they get fresh air. The headache pulsing behind her eyes was bad, but not migraine bad. The water had helped, was helping, which was why she continued to drink even as they made their way down a hill and around toward the lake.

When they broke free of the trees, she looked up to find the moon shining down on them. A beautiful full moon that lit the lake with soft, feathery light. A small dock was nearby, with a moored rowboat. The white paint of the dock was wearing away, as if they'd stepped into the past. "It's beautiful," she whispered, letting herself slip free of the terror of the last few hours and embrace the clear, crisp night. The water lapped gently against the rocks and tempted her to take off her shoes and dip her toes in. "It's perfect."

"A bit of sanctuary amid the madness. A perfect escape."

The comment made it through her defenses. For a moment, a brief moment, she forgot where they were. And who he was.

"You created the madness," she observed. "One you could walk away from if you chose to."

Was that a laugh? "Life's not that easy for some of us, Doc. Sorry—Ashley." He held up his hands in surrender. "Not a soap fan. I forgot. Does your husband like soap operas?"

"My husband? Oh, um, yes, actually. He loves—"

He shook his head and even in the moonlit night, she could see humor in his eyes. "You still haven't gotten that down. You know what I think?"

"I haven't the faintest—"

He hooked an arm around her waist and pulled

her close, dipped his head until his lips were a mere breath from hers. "I bet you don't have a husband. You have something. A friend. Cousin. Brother?" He looked deep into her eyes. "Ah. Brother. Jack's your brother." That self-satisfied smirk on his face should have set off alarm bells, but she stayed right where she was, pressed against him, hands gripping his shoulders. Why was she so drawn to him? Why wasn't she afraid of him? Why did being in his arms feel like the perfect place to be? "That means I can finally do this."

She opened her mouth to protest but instead found his hot, demanding mouth on hers. Her mind emptied of every thought, every strategy she'd made, and refilled in an instant with him. The strength of him, the taut muscles beneath the T-shirt, the smooth way his arms cradled her. Desire punched through reason. When he angled his head to the side, the pressure changed, tempted, as he dived in and took what she only now realized she wanted to give.

His tongue dueled with hers, teased her into surrender even as she clung to him, inhaling the scent of the night air along with the spicy scent of citrus and pine. The haze in her head threatened to take her over completely as his hold on her loosened. He lifted his mouth, not much. Not far. But enough for her to lower her chin and press her forehead against his chest.

"Definitely not married." His hands slipped to her hips, his fingers resting lightly against her. She took a shaky breath, felt her heart hammering so hard she couldn't hear the water any longer. "How about we try that again?"

She leaned back, lifted her eyes to his, and for an instant, regret swept over her before it passed. "Let's say we do…" She reached both hands up, diving her fingers into the thickness of his hair as he bent to kiss her again. In one fast move, she held his head down and brought up her knee. She miscalculated, hit him in the stomach before bringing her knee up again and connecting this time. His head snapped back and he landed hard on the ground. She stood there for a moment, her mind screaming at her to do the one thing she'd been waiting to do for hours.

She ran.

Chapter 6

Slade groaned, pressing a hand to his temple as he rolled onto his side. He'd known she was up to something. At least, that's what Slade told himself as he waited for his head to stop spinning.

As smart as Dr. Ashley McTavish was, she was a horrible liar and an even worse sneak. If she'd been fooling anyone with that whole "I want to wash his blood off my hands" disclaimer, it had only been herself. Spying on her stuffing protein bars into her pockets when she thought no one was looking might have been comical if the stakes weren't so high. But her attempted deception had given him an idea. An idea that took an unexpected turn when she'd plowed her knee into first his stomach, then his forehead.

He heard her crashing through the brush. If she'd wanted to get somewhere, she should have stuck to the perimeter of the lake, not diving blindly into the darkness of the forest. Slade pushed himself up, half expecting to find cartoon canaries circling his head. She'd clobbered him for sure and even earned a bit of his admiration, but that quickly dissipated when he heard the front door of the cabin being slammed shut.

Lucky hustled along the trail Ashley had inadvertently created. He followed the narrow stomped path, listening not only for her scrambling, but for her breathing. Sprinting like that was going to exhaust her sooner than later, a benefit to him as he heard Badger calling his name.

It could have been worse. It could have been Olena who had gotten curious, Slade told himself. He paced himself, moving away from the cabin, his eyes adjusting to the dark. The moonlight barely penetrated the branches. The scent of damp earth and recent rain caught his attention, had him angling off to the east. The last thing he wanted to do was bring attention to the fact she'd gotten away from him. He was already creating some ridiculous fiction as to why they'd left the lake when he took her back to the cabin. And she would be going back. He could already feel a shift in the trust factor.

Olena had flicked a look at Slade when she and

Ashley had been discussing trust. He needed to earn some of that trust back if he was going to get Ashley out of here safely and keep his cover in place.

He needed to get Valeri to that meeting on the docks with Edik. He refused to consider that the past eighteen months would be a waste. For almost two years his cousin Georgiana had been missing without a word. He understood Ashley's determination to get away, but doing so now would work against Slade. And that, unfortunately, he couldn't allow.

His foot crunched down on something odd. He stopped, crouched and brushed debris aside. A protein bar. He picked it up, shoved it in his back pocket and continued… Wait. He turned, looking closely at the trees and surrounding flora. No one had broken through here. Her trail ended. Just stopped cold.

Had she backtracked? Had she somehow circled around him and headed to the lake? He didn't think so. She wasn't that sneaky. Or that careful. A rustle of leaves had him looking up and, after blinking a few times, he could see her shadow stretched across a branch far above him. Relief mingled with irritation. What on earth was she thinking?

He was about to call up to her, but he stopped himself. Climbing up after her was an option, one he didn't particularly like. That left option number two.

Slade dropped down and sat at the base of the tree, reached behind him for the protein bar and ripped open the package. It was a good time for a snack considering it was looking as if she was going to be keeping him on constant alert. Too bad the bar tasted like sawdust.

The branch creaked. Ashley didn't strike him as outdoorsy. He'd lay good money down she hadn't climbed a tree since she was a kid, if then. The odds she'd found a secure branch in the time she'd had, that she'd managed to situate herself in a way she could stay up there indefinitely, were about as good as his swimming across the Pacific.

"When you're ready to come down, give me a heads-up, would you?" He didn't have to shout. Not in the stillness of the night. "I've already got a headache from where you kneed me. I don't particularly want to add to it."

"Stupid protein bar," she muttered.

He took another bite of the ridiculously named peanut butter bar.

"Are you going to shoot me down?" she whispered.

"I don't have my gun."

"Liar."

Truer words were never spoken. "Don't ever forget it."

"Can't you just let me go? Tell them you lost me."

"I could. But I'd prefer to keep breathing." It was, perhaps, the most honest statement he'd made to her. "If we're gone for much longer, they're going to suspect something's wrong."

"Something is wrong." She shifted against the branches. "I'm stuck."

Slade dropped his head back against the tree, unable to stop the smile from forming. "Tell me another one."

"No, I mean it. I can't… Oh, wait. There. I think I've… Whoa!"

Slade shot to his feet as the bottom half of her dropped down. She hung there, a good ten feet over his head, feet dangling. "How did you get up that far?"

"Adrenaline. I wasn't thinking of how to get down at the time."

He tossed the bar aside and positioned himself under her. "Let go."

"Are you crazy?"

"Ashley, let go. I'll catch you."

"I'll flatten you like a Sunday-morning pancake."

"Then you'll be on your way again. Let go, Ashley." He reached his arms up. "Drop. Now."

"Don't you have a rope or something on you? Something I could shimmy… Oh!" The branch snapped. She dropped. And landed right on top of him. He caught her, but not before he lost his balance and set them both toppling to the ground, the renegade branch landing across both their legs. He lay there, on his back, Ashley sprawled on top of him, her blond hair catching a ray of moonlight that set her to glowing. "That was easier than I thought.

Are you hurt?" She slid her doctor's hands across his torso, making him suck in a breath so hard his back teeth ached.

"Only my pride." He sighed and stood up, more than a bit surprised she didn't scramble away from him like a scared pup. "You?" A thin line of blood trickled down her cheek.

"A few scrapes, nothing more. Let's go." She grabbed his hand and shoved to her feet, but he stood where he was.

"No."

"But we can get away. We have a head start—"

"Lucky? Ashley?"

"Badger." Slade tugged her back in the direction they had come from. "We need to go back. Now."

"They are going to kill me!" She struggled against his hold. "You know that."

"I won't let them. Ashley, believe me. You are safer with me than you are out there on your own."

"I'll take my chances." She kicked at his shins, but he was on to her this time and dodged the blow.

"Stop it! Olena is just waiting for you to make a break for it. She wants you to!"

"Happy to oblige." She twisted to break his hold, but he didn't let go. He couldn't. The second he did, she was dead. And so was he.

"You have no idea what that woman is capable of, Ashley." His serious words broke through. She stopped fighting him, her breathing ragged as she stared at him. "I promise you, you have a chance if you stick with me."

"Then let's keep going." Her eyes lit with hope. "You can help me get away. I'll tell the police—they'll believe what I tell them." A branch snapped behind them before a beam of light cut through the darkness. "My brother—"

Slade dragged her against him just in time.

"Don't mean to interrupt." Badger lounged against a tree and looked less intimidating than his namesake. He flicked the flashlight on and off like a kid with a new toy. "Thought you were taking a walk by the lake…"

"We wanted more privacy. Right, Dr. Ashley?" When he released her, she shoved him away. Hard. Hard enough those cartoon canaries nearly appeared. The anger, the frustration, the fear on her face hit him right in the gut even as he realized her reaction was exactly what they needed. "Right. Guess maybe our moonlit stroll is over." He motioned for Badger to go on ahead of them. "You lead, Badger. We're right behind you."

"Whatever you say, Lucky." Badger's sly grin was still on his face when they got back to the cabin.

"What happened?" Olena was waiting for them on the porch, that blade of hers securely in her palm. "She run? Tell me she ran."

Slade stepped in front of Ashley. "I took care of it. It won't happen again. Right, Doctor?"

Ashley walked toward the cabin, but Olena stood nose to nose with her.

Seconds later, Ashley pushed Olena aside and climbed the rest of the stairs. "I've had a rough day. We can play later."

"Oh, burn!" Badger said from the open front door as he stepped aside to let Ashley enter.

Olena whipped around and sent the blade flying. It hit the frame inches from Badger's face. "You're all expendable," she seethed, tossing a look at Slade. "We don't need any of you." In that moment, Slade knew precisely what he had to do. Case or not, eighteen months or not, he had to get out and take Ashley with him.

"If you're going to sleep this close to me, can you at least turn off your brain?" Ashley flopped onto her back and nearly caught Sawyer in the face. She didn't apologize for it. She wasn't going to apologize for anything. She couldn't believe he'd dragged her back here. Couldn't believe he hadn't let her go. So much for her big plan that relied on his wanting her to be safe.

"I'm thinking."

"No kidding. I can hear the wheels grinding." She stared up at the ceiling.

"Get some sleep, Ashley."

She recognized that tone. He was just about at the end of his rope with her. The resignation. The frustration. It was a tone she'd elicited frequently over the years. From her ex-husband especially. "What are you thinking about?"

"Right now? I'm considering locking you in the bathroom so I can figure stuff out."

She smirked, rolled onto her side and looked at him. Even in the darkness he was a striking figure. In other circumstances she'd have considered him attractive. She didn't have vast experience when it came to men, she admitted. And her sex life with Adam for the few years they were married had been…adequate. Not adequate enough for him, given he had cheated on her. A lot. So yeah, maybe when it came to men her judgment was a bit off. That didn't mean she couldn't appreciate Lucky— no, Sawyer—from his shaggy, too-long brown hair, to his tight, toned, tattooed body, to his complicated character. Wow, she was starting to lose all common sense, wasn't she? She tucked her hands under her cheek. "What are you really thinking about?"

"This might have escaped your notice, but this is not a slumber party and I am not a twelve-year-old girl."

Oh, she knew. Especially the last bit. "Back in the woods. When you held me close. I assume that was to throw Badger off the scent?"

"Clearly it didn't work."

"You wanted Badger to think we'd gone out there for something other than to look at the lake?"

"No one thought we were looking at the lake." He turned his head, his hair rustling on the pillow. Even in the darkness, she knew he was looking at her. "If Badger had heard me guess about your brother, he'd have done something about it right then and there. You understand me, Ashley?"

She swallowed hard. He was right, of course. "Jack can help you, Lu—Sawyer," she corrected quickly. "I promise he'll listen to me. If you help me, I'll tell him. He can get you a reduced sentence." The urge to touch him overwhelmed her and she reached out and laid a gentle hand on his chest. "He'd talk to the judge. Or the DA. I know one in the Sacramento office. Simone would listen to me, too. You don't have to stay with Valeri. There's another way."

While still looking at her, he lifted a hand and covered hers. "There's not another way for me, Ashley. I'm where I am because I chose it. And while I appreciate the offer of leniency, you can't promise anything. Because of me, a prison guard is dead. Whatever happens down the road, I'm in for life. And you need to stop seeing me as if I'm some misunderstood victim who is worthy of redemption. I'm not."

"Everyone's worthy of— Well, maybe not *everyone*." She brushed a hand over his forehead. "I'm sorry I hurt you."

He took her hand away. "Don't."

"Don't what? Don't touch you?" But she wanted to. In the worst way. She didn't even care if it was wrong.

"Don't go making me out to be something I'm not. I'm not a knight on a white horse. I am not a good man. No matter how much you want to pretend."

"I bet you're a better one than you think." How did he read her so well? "And I'll pretend as long as it keeps me sane." And that, she told herself, was what she was doing. "I have to have something to hold on to, Sawyer. I need to find hope somewhere. Otherwise I'm going to drown in the fear. I won't surrender to it without fighting. Right now, you're all I've got."

"It almost sounds like you trust me." He lifted their clasped hands to his mouth, pressed a kiss against her fingers.

"Maybe I do." And she still couldn't explain why.

"Then let me think." He released her hand and rolled her away from him, but before he moved out of reach, she grabbed his arm, pulled it across her and clung. "Not the best position for thinking."

"Shut up." Ashley grinned and snuggled back against him until she could feel his body curled around hers. "If you're here, I can sleep. And maybe you can, too."

"I seriously doubt it."

There it was again, the irritation, but he didn't leave her. Instead, he tightened his hold on her and tucked her close.

And that was enough. For now.

"I understand you explored the woods last night."

Ashley remained steady as she took Valeri's pulse, checked his heartbeat and blood pressure. Her patient surprised her. And not in a good way. If she believed in superhuman powers, she'd have thought his was to heal himself far faster than she'd have liked. Already he'd been walking around the room, regaining his strength, not to mention his color. That he was sitting up in bed, with stitches both inside and outside his body, had her marveling at the ability of the human body. And the mind that controlled it.

"The weather was nice," Ashley said finally. "And I was feeling cooped up."

"You are responsible for the bruise on Lucky's forehead."

"Yep." She wasn't about to apologize for trying to save her own life. "Going to add that to my list of sins?"

"I'm partial to sins." Valeri pushed himself farther up against the headboard. "You have spirit, Dr. Ashley."

"Enough you're going to let me live?"

Whatever humor had been dancing in Valeri's eyes faded.

"How about you do me a favor?" Ashley asked. "When the time comes, I'd appreciate it if it isn't Olena who does the deed. It doesn't seem right to reward her for such rude behavior where I'm concerned."

Valeri's burst of laughter surprised her. "It has always been difficult for my daughter to make friends. I would blame myself, but it is a quality that makes her very effective."

His daughter? Even with that unexpected tidbit

of information, it did not escape Ashley's notice they were joking about her own forthcoming demise. Sawyer's midnight musings had resulted in a plan of sorts, one that required both of them to cause some friction among the different personalities who were beginning to suffer from a serious bout of cabin fever. The other was for Ashley to endear herself—however much she was comfortable with—to Valeri. He was the only one capable of controlling Olena.

Now she knew why.

She'd already caused a blowup between Javi and Badger when she'd asked who had wrecked the video game console. She had, of course, but she'd made sure to do so after Badger had been futzing with it. They were now going stir-crazy and she was happy to help exacerbate the symptoms.

Olena and Taras had been gone since early morning on a run to restock supplies. They were the only ones whose faces were not plastered all over the news and social media. Even Ashley had become a media star, the innocent Good Samaritan doctor who had been abducted after stopping to help the crash survivors.

If she'd had any doubt about executing Sawyer's plan, it had vanished when she'd seen the picture of prison guard Bradley Sherman, and heard that he'd left behind a pregnant wife along with his parents and three siblings. Sawyer had said it was his fault the guard had been killed, but Ashley knew better. It was hers. She'd pushed too far and Valeri had turned his anger on Bradley instead. At least, that's how it played out in her nightmares. She owed it to Bradley, or at least his memory, to stay alive.

"So Olena is your daughter."

"She is."

"And Taras? He's not your son."

"Nephew. The oldest son of my oldest brother. It is a family business."

A business she still didn't know about. She was running out of ideas to keep herself useful now that Valeri was on the mend. As she packed up her bag, she scanned the room, her gaze landing on the small table by the window. And the chessboard sitting atop it. "Do you play?"

Valeri sighed. "I do. I'm afraid none of my current companions offer much of a challenge, however." He eyed her, clearly suspicious.

"I was district champion for two years in high school. I haven't played in a while, though." She looked up, widened her eyes. "Would you like a game?"

"I would indeed."

"Outside? In the—"

"In the fresh air?" He finished with something akin to amusement in his pale eyes.

"Don't worry." She made it a point to sound contrite as she retrieved the game. "Lucky made certain I learned my lesson."

"Let us hope so."

* * *

"I am getting sick of sandwiches," Badger grumbled and tossed the half-eaten bologna on the kitchen table. "When are we getting out of here?"

Slade looked up from the laptop, feigning irritation. "You keep whining like that and you'll get out sooner than the rest of us."

Badger kicked at the chair next to him. "This wasn't part of the deal."

"No," Javi said from the sofa in the next room. "But it was part of the plan. You helped Valeri get him the items he needed—he got you out. Once he's gone, you can be about your business. Until then, keep quiet!"

Badger shot to his feet and stomped around the room. "I gotta breathe. I gotta get out of this place."

"So take a walk." Slade returned his attention to the laptop and his unsuccessful attempts to access the secured dark-net website to report in. Between prying eyes and a program on the machine that tracked every keystroke, there was no way to make contact with Baxter and his team. He could only hope the chance he'd taken leaving a note on Clive's phone meant the FBI would be there for the meet.

"Can I take a walk with your girlfriend?" Badger leaned his hands on the table and stared down the hallway to Ashley's room.

It took a lot to make Slade forget his training, but Badger and Javi's bickering managed to push him right to the edge. "I don't think so."

Badger swept his hands across the table and dislodged Javi's solitaire game.

"You jerk." Javi stood up and reached out his one good arm. When Badger danced out of the man's reach, Javi bent down to retrieve his cards. "Go play outside."

"He can go play later." Olena came in from the front porch, Taras and Valeri right behind her. "They're still searching so we won't move until they move on. Two, maybe three days."

"Two more days?" Badger whined. "Are you freaking kidding me?"

Olena glanced at Slade. "You going to protect him, too?"

"No." Slade shook his head, closed the laptop. He wouldn't have a chance to warn Baxter about Valeri's schedule. His hope was fading fast. At least no one had taken to following him on his walks down to the dock, where he'd been stashing supplies, clothes, one of the burner phones and emergency items in a waterproof duffel. If things went sideways, he wanted a plan in place for a quick getaway. "He's all yours."

Olena reached behind her for her knife and sent it soaring. Badger ducked just in time. The knife sliced into the wall. The sick smile on Olena's lips had Slade notching up his worry.

"Enough." Valeri sighed and lowered himself into the chair beside Slade. "You are worse than naughty children on the playground. Where is the doctor?"

"In her room." Slade didn't like how Valeri asked about her.

"She will be coming with us."

"No!" Olena was furious.

Valeri didn't blink. "We have clients who will value her skills."

Slade's stomach churned but he sat back as Olena's rage grew. "I will not allow it."

Valeri's response was in Russian and shot out of his mouth, but Slade had spent enough time around him that he got the gist. Olena was being overruled. And she was not happy about it.

One of the cell phones on the table buzzed awake. It buzzed again. And a third time. Taras reached for it then, but Valeri held up his hand. "That is the warning." The phone went silent again. "He will call back at the scheduled time. Two days," he told them before shifting to face Javi. "We will leave in two days. All of us. Now deal me in."

"Appreciate you letting me stay here," Eamon told Eden Delaney as she cleaned the crumbs from their pizza dinner off her kitchen counter. One thing about being on a big case—his eating habits went from not great to downright awful. That was when he remembered to eat at all. "I wasn't looking forward to a hotel." His partner, on the other hand, had been chomping at the bit, and declared her intention of making use of the hotel gym and pool the second she checked in. While Eamon had been spending more time in the valley, his assigned city was still a little more than ninety minutes away in San Francisco.

"Between our loft and Jack's, we have plenty of room. Family doesn't stay in a hotel." Eden whipped her strawberry blonde hair over her shoulder. "And as hard as it is for you to accept, that's what you are."

He toasted her with his water, choosing to let the comment slide. It was still difficult, after all these years, to move beyond the past that linked him, Eden, DA Simone Sutton and Dr. Allie Kellan. His sister, Chloe, had been a light in all their lives, a light that had been snuffed out before she'd turned ten. Eamon had drifted apart from them in so many ways, but the three women had refused to let him slip away. Chloe's death—her murder— had set them all on various paths, but in the end, when they'd finally caught Chloe's killer more than twenty years after the fact, he'd found himself glad to have their company. No questions. No regrets. He'd just felt…welcomed.

Because he needed to focus on a different topic, he asked, "Cole still keeping the boat?"

"Oh, yeah." Eden beamed. "I wouldn't let him get rid of it. Chloe Ann was conceived on that boat."

"Ah, geez, Eden." Eamon squeezed his eyes shut.

"You know I still think of you like a little sister. Why do you say things like that?"

"Because of reactions like that." Eden's laugh drifted through the spacious modern kitchen, then expanded when Cole strolled in with three-month-old Chloe Ann—Eamon's sister's namesake—in his arms. "There's my girl. And my guy." Eden stopped and just looked at them. "What a picture, huh?"

Eamon had to admit they were and, not for the first time, he wondered what Chloe's life would have been like if she'd lived. Would she be married by now? Have a baby?

"Chloe Ann would like to see Uncle Eamon." Cole passed her off to Eamon before heading to the fridge. "And she would like a bottle."

Eamon stared down at the wiggling infant currently clad in a bulging diaper and a bright blue onesie that declared her mistress of the universe.

"She's not going to break. Or explode." Eden came over and readjusted infant and honorary uncle until Chloe Ann was settled in his arms, blinking fascinated eyes up at him. "There you go. Ah, finally. Freedom." She spun over to Cole and planted a kiss on his smiling lips. "Now that she's suitably distracted, you two can tell me what's going on with finding Ashley. What's up with this Slade Palmer agent? You find anything on him? What about the phone?"

Eamon looked down at his sister's namesake and tapped a finger against the dimple in her cheek.

"Your mama thinks I'm going to spill company secrets because you're so cute. Did you know that?" Chloe Ann cooed and drooled, kicked her bare feet like she was paddling.

"Or you could just tell Chloe," Eden suggested. "We can eavesdrop."

"Eden, don't," Cole warned.

"Don't what?" Eden said, taking the bottle from Cole and setting it in simmering water on the stove. "You already told me Palmer's an FBI agent undercover with the gang. That's good news, right?"

"Near as we can tell. His record is spotless." But that was all before he'd spent the last two years in a kind of chaos Eamon couldn't begin to imagine. "As far as the phone goes…" He looked to Cole for an answer to that question.

"Jason's still working on it," Cole said. "If he hasn't cracked the password or print protection by morning, we'll get Tammy at the lab on it."

Eamon nodded. Jason Sutton, Vince's younger brother, had an eerie knack with anything digital, which came in handy now that he worked with Vince as a private investigator. Personally, Eamon hoped Jason cracked the phone as he didn't relish the idea of taking it anywhere official like the Sac Metro lab. Eamon himself was already stretching the rules thinner than he had in the past. One day his luck was going to run out.

"The better news would be better news if we knew where they were." Eamon watched Eden set the timer on her smartwatch. "You really use that thing to do more than tell time?"

"Sadly, yes. I'm addicted," Eden admitted.

"Lets me keep in contact with her when she's working a case." Cole drew her in for a hug. "Not sure if it would find her in a meat locker, though."

Eden frowned. "Are you ever going to let me forget that?"

Cole kissed her nose. "Nope."

Eamon had been regaled by the story of Eden's capture by the Iceman, a serial killer who had left his victims in vacant meat lockers. The details shifted depending on who was telling the story, but the ending was thankfully always the same: happily-ever-after.

"Tracking your wife at work," Eamon said to Cole as he grabbed a bottle of beer out of the fridge. "That doesn't exactly scream romance."

"It's all a matter of perspective, my friend. Oh, and as for perspective, that agent Baxter of yours, he's a bit cold."

"He definitely has the whole stay-detached thing down." Eamon, on the other hand, tended to be too involved in his cases. If he wasn't careful, in the not too distant future, he was going to burn out. He watched Chloe Ann become fascinated with his nose. He needed to make some changes before that came to pass.

"You should get one," Eden said.

"A baby?" Eamon didn't mean to sound quite so strangled.

"One of those, too." Eden shot Cole a look Eamon didn't miss. "But I was talking about the watch. Lots of stuff you can do with it."

"Like tell time?" Eamon lifted his arm to point at his simple wristwatch. "Got that covered." The last thing he needed was his mother finding a way to keep track of…him. "Oh, no. No, no, no." His mind exploded and he held out Chloe Ann to a startled Eden. "Sorry. I can't believe we didn't think of this before." He got out his phone and called Jack, who happened to live upstairs from Eden and Cole. "Jack…Yeah, sorry. I know it's late…No, I don't have any news." He flinched. He should have figured that would be Jack's first thought when he saw that he was calling. "Does Ashley have a watch? I mean, a smartwatch?" Hope surged through him at the answer. "Okay, great… No…Yeah. I have an idea. I need to call Baxter and bring him in on this, but if it works…Okay, meet me downstairs in five."

"Eamon, what's going on?" Eden asked when he quit the call.

"You don't recognize that look?" Cole asked.

"It just dawned on me," Eamon said. "Those smartwatches come with GPS, don't they?"

"Some do," Eden confirmed. "Through the owner's cell phone, though."

"Ashley's cell was destroyed," Cole reminded him.

"Maybe. And if we can't get anything from it,

we can access her dashboard account. It's worth a shot. I need to call Agent Baxter and Sarah. The more eyes we have on this the better. Keep a good thought," he called to them and raced out the front door.

Chapter 7

"Everyone tucked in bed?" Ashley asked Slade as he lay down beside her. Oddly, she'd looked forward to this time. She'd ignored his warning and continued to believe there was far more decency about him than he wanted her to think. He even insisted on sleeping above the blankets while she burrowed beneath them.

"There's plenty of room on your side, Ashley." His voice drifted through the darkness and when she inched closer to rest her head on his shoulder, he tensed.

"I know." She smothered a yawn. "But the closer I am, the more I can whisper. Why didn't you tell me Olena is Valeri's daughter?"

The silence stretched paper thin. "How did you find out?"

"Valeri's a lot more chatty than you'd give him credit for. Especially while playing chess. At least with someone he considers inferior." It still burned her that she'd let him win. Placating a psychopath was more difficult on the ego than she'd expected.

"The man's a fool if he thinks that of you."

What a sweet—and unexpected—thing for him to say. "He also said that Taras is his nephew. Oldest son of his oldest brother. Sounds like one big happy family."

"It sounds like something, all right." He scooted toward the edge of the bed. She moved closer. "Ashley—"

"They're expecting something. A signal, I think. Olena came over when we were playing chess. Started talking in Russian, but she tapped a finger on her watch. I pretended not to notice. What's he done? Valeri."

"Lots of things, but in this case it's human trafficking."

She wasn't sure what she thought she'd hear, although she wasn't surprised by Sawyer's answer. She'd worked in ERs long enough to treat patients who had suffered all types of traumas. But exploitation was close to the worst thing one person could do to another.

"His organization has a wide customer base and

he's very, very good at it. I hate him for it. I'd kill him if I could."

"And yet you're going along with all this." Nausea churned in her stomach, rose into her throat even as she heard the regret in his tone.

"I told you I was not a good man. And as for Valeri, people are disposable to him, Ashley. They're nothing more than profit and loss."

She should move away from him. She should get up and sleep in the chair. She should shatter that window and run, and whatever happened when they caught her happened. But she didn't move. Instead, she flattened her palm against his chest and felt his heart beat beneath her hand. "Why do you spend so much time trying to scare me?"

"Because you need to be scared." He set her arm at her side and sat up. "You keep trying to see the good in everyone. Good that isn't always there. Stop romanticizing this situation. It's only going to mess with your head."

She lay there, unable to reason out the odd emotions and thoughts rioting through her mind. "I am scared. I've been scared from the moment the bus crashed. But I can't dwell on it. Doing so means I'm already dead." She sat up, too, and slipped her arms around him from behind. "The only time I'm not scared is when I'm with you."

He dropped his chin to his chest, covered one of her hands with his. "Ashley…"

"I can only judge a person based on my experience with them. I'm not naive, Sawyer. I know you've done some horrible things, but you've also done good. You've kept me safe." She shivered, and not from being cold. She couldn't process her feelings any longer; she'd tried, was exhausted. The bottom line was that the man he was with her wasn't the man he purported to be. "I live in the real world and I know what's going on around me. I know what's coming for me and that you probably can't protect me from it." He looked over his shoulder at her and, even in the darkness, she saw the uncertainty on his face. She caught his chin between her fingers, turned him so he had to face her completely. "My heart sees you, Sawyer. You." She captured his face between her palms. "The good and the bad. But mostly the good." She pressed her lips to his.

"I can't do this," he whispered against her mouth. "Don't make me—"

"Don't let me die without having made love with you."

"He's not going to kill you, Ashley." He pressed his forehead against hers. "He's going to find a buyer."

It was the way he said it, the quiet desperation, the barely hidden anger. His concern and fear put them on a far more equal footing than he probably realized. She kissed him then because it was the only response she had that didn't involve a soul-wracking scream. She clung to him, pressed her lips to his and took what she wanted, what she needed, in this frightening moment.

His hands caressed her back, her shoulders, until he held her hips and hauled her onto him. She straddled him, felt his hard, aroused strength pressing against her core. She rocked, rose, unable to tear her mouth from his as their tongues touched, entwined, mated. Her entire body tingled as his fingers roamed up beneath the hem of her sweater to the clasp of her bra.

She couldn't hear anything over the sound of their hard, heavy breaths that couldn't catch. She wanted him. She needed him. If only to forget the promise of the horror waiting on the other side of that door. When Sawyer's palms brushed against the sides of her breasts, she gasped, lifted her head and groaned.

"Not enough," he said, his voice rough. As she dragged her sweater over her head, he brushed his hot mouth against the swell of her breasts. She arched toward him, desire shooting through her like an arrow of fire, igniting every inch of her body. "Ashley." Her name on his lips was the most wondrous sound she'd ever heard and the only thing she wanted to hear.

Desperate to feel his bare flesh, she tugged his shirt off, teased his skin with her teeth and tongue. He reciprocated, teasing her to the point that the juncture between her thighs pulsed with promise.

She sighed. She sobbed. And when he leaned forward, putting her onto her back, she moaned.

The sight of him above her left her hovering in a place where she didn't want to be alone. Ashley held out her hand. He slipped his fingers through hers, then stopped.

"Condom."

"Ashley." She grinned. "My name is Ashley."

He looked for a moment as if confused, but then he laughed, turned to her medical bag and extricated the foil packets.

"Come back over here." When he did, she sat up and he drew her into his arms and kissed her again.

The door burst open.

Ashley screamed and grabbed for the blanket just as Sawyer moved to push her behind him.

"Taras?" Sawyer's entire body had tensed. The light flashed on. Olena and Valeri came into the room. She'd never seen such grim faces. "Valeri, what's going on?"

Olena reached past Sawyer for Ashley and grabbed at her wrist. Sawyer intervened but—

"Enough!" Valeri ordered.

Ashley felt faint. She'd realized what they might be looking for.

"Your watch. Where is it?" Olena demanded.

Fear coiled inside Ashley like a rattler. "What watch?" She had to try. There were guns pointed at not just her, but Sawyer, too.

Olena dragged her from the bed.

"All right. Okay." Sawyer lifted his hands in surrender. "Just let us get dressed. We can talk this out. Whatever is going on, I'm sure we can—"

Taras cocked his weapon.

"Bring them." Valeri stalked out of the room.

Ashley, unable to make a sound, the terror so great, dropped to the floor and threw her sweater on and grabbed her shoes, held them against her chest as Olena steered her out of the bedroom. "Sawyer?"

Taras waggled the gun for Sawyer to get his shirt. "Olena was right about you. Your priorities are all mixed up. Move."

Olena's grip felt like an iron vise as she pulled Ashley past Javi and Badger in the hallway. The pair looked as if they'd also been roused from bed by the commotion.

Valeri was waiting outside. "Get dressed. All of you. We're leaving."

At first Ashley thought he was talking to her. Apparently so did Olena since she released Ashley's arm.

"Why are we changing the plan?" Javi asked.

"Put your shoes on, Ashley," Sawyer whispered when he was shoved over to stand beside her. He pulled on his T-shirt. She shoved her bare feet into her sneakers.

"What's happening?" she asked him, only to get a short shake of his head in response. Thick raindrops began to fall, only a few at first, but then more. Faster. Harder.

"We need to leave. Now!" Valeri's voice was forced calm. "They're tracking her through her watch."

"I don't have a watch." Ashley wasn't sure how the lie sounded.

Taras pointed the barrel of his gun in Sawyer's direction. "Where is it?"

There was no joke that Ashley could try now that would tamp down the fear surging through her. "In the bathroom. Behind the picture next to the sink."

"I knew it." Olena stormed into the house.

"It doesn't work without my phone," Ashley defended herself by taking a page out of Sawyer's playbook. "Olena said she destroyed it."

"The Feds have work-arounds." Badger yawned and turned for the cabin. Javi jogged past him.

It seemed like only minutes before they filed out of the cabin with their things. Badger brought up the rear, a jacket half on, half off, lugging a giant duffel behind him.

Valeri nodded, then glared at Sawyer and held his gaze. "You left her phone on in the car."

"What? No!" Ashley stepped forward to place herself between the two men, but Sawyer didn't waver. He was, just as he'd been that night on the bus, an immovable force. "It was me, not—"

"Be quiet, Ashley." Sawyer's voice had turned as serious as Valeri's. "This doesn't have anything to do with the watch." The utter calm she heard baffled her. What was really going on? "Or the phone. Does it, Valeri? How long have you known?"

Valeri nodded. "Not long."

"Know? Know what?" Ashley demanded. Why did it seem as if everyone understood what was playing out except her? She moved to get around Sawyer, but he trapped her behind him.

Valeri's eyes narrowed on them as Badger pulled the van to a screeching halt in front of the cabin.

"Run." Sawyer didn't look at her. Didn't bother to keep his voice down.

"Where?" she whispered.

"You know where."

The lake, she thought. The other night he'd called it the perfect escape.

"Go, Ashley. Now."

She hesitated, not able to believe him.

"Go!"

Ashley ran, her feet barely touching the ground as she sped down the path. Shots rang out behind her, but she didn't stop. Didn't dare. Voices shouted, but she could hear little beyond the pounding of her heart. She slipped and slid on the dock, racing over to the boat, her fingers going numb as she tried to untie the rope knot that kept it moored. More shouts. The gunning of an engine. Two shots. Three. No, four.

Ashley gasped, looking behind her, waiting, hoping. Praying.

She recognized the shape of the shadow that burst into view. Sawyer had a gun in his hand, one he tucked into the back of his jeans as he sprinted toward the dock.

"Get in!" he ordered and flinched, pressed a hand against his side.

"You're hurt."

"I'm fine. Hurry."

He crouched down, dragged up a rope that had something attached. A duffel bobbed to the surface. He finished untying the rope knot as she jumped into the boat. She grabbed for the oars and began to row the second he joined her, yanking the strap of the duffel bag over his head. Her arms burned; her shoulders ached. She grunted as she slipped the oars as quickly as she could through the still surface of the water. Her feet went cold, as if they were in ice. She looked down and in the moonlight saw water collecting in the bottom of the boat.

"Sawyer?"

He twisted around to look behind them. To where Olena and Taras stood on the edge of the dock. Olena waved her weapon at them.

Ashley summoned what courage she had left and tried to row faster, but the boat was filling with water, making it even heavier.

"Can you swim?" Sawyer asked her.

"Yes."

"Good. Swim for shore. As fast as you can."

"But—" The shore seemed miles away. She'd only swum laps in a pool. And not recently.

"It's either swim there or drown here. Not great odds, I'm afraid."

"Right." She dropped the oars, stood up and dived into the water. The ice-cold temperature shocked her mind empty. Her arms and legs flailed, and it took more effort than expected to surface. When she did, she saw Sawyer waiting for the boat to fill, then he dived into the lake. When he popped up beside her, she could see he didn't approve of her decision to wait, but seeing him, she swam on, pushing through the pain in her body, focusing on stroke after stroke, breath after breath.

"You okay?" Sawyer called to her and she stopped. He came up beside her, his face pale in the moonlight as he treaded water.

"Yeah." She choked on a mouthful of water. "You?"

"I'll be fine," he repeated. "We need to keep moving."

"We need to find a phone and call my brother," Ashley corrected.

"We won't find one in the lake," Sawyer said. "Swim for the other side. We'll find someplace eventually."

She kicked into gear, wondering if she was ever going to feel safe again. Ashley lost track of time. Her lungs burned as if they'd been set on fire. She should be worried that she couldn't feel her toes or her fingers. When she kicked and felt ground catch against her shoe, she sobbed in relief, sprinting the rest of the way until she dropped onto the shore, coughing and gasping as every bit of her dripped water.

"Sawyer?" Her voice sounded hoarse. She sat back on her heels and looked behind her. He was a fair distance away, moving more slowly than she'd have thought. Ashley shoved to her feet, her knees wobbling as she stepped back into the water and shouted for him. "You're almost there! Come on!" But he was gasping for air and for a horrifying moment, he sank out of sight.

Panic seized her. It was pitch-black. Not even the moon cast light on this side of the shore. No homes nearby, no lights or guideposts. How would she ever find him?

But she would. He would not leave her like this. She would not lose him. Not now. She waded into the water, stumbled, nearly fell face-first, just as he surfaced. He took a moment to retch, his hand clutching his side as he slowly moved toward her, water cascading from the bag on his hip.

"What is it?" She'd seen enough injuries to know something was seriously wrong. She wedged herself under his arm and helped him walk the rest of the way to dry land. "Where are you hurt?"

"Doesn't matter," he wheezed as he dropped to the ground. He leaned back, still pressing a hand to his side. Blood soaked through his shirt and onto his fingers. "I'll be fine in a minute. We need to get moving."

She dragged his shirt up, tried to examine the wound. "I can't see anything other than blood."

"I know." He covered her hand with his, squeezed her fingers. "Ashley, listen to me. Valeri left with Badger and Olena, but he ordered Taras and Javi to stay behind. They're coming after me, Ashley."

"Us. They're coming after us. Let me—"

"No. It's me they want. Which means you're in even more danger than you were before. You need to go on alone. Now. While it's still dark."

"I'm not leaving you." She slung his arm over her shoulders and, with enough effort that her feet sank into the dirt, helped him up. He let out a sound that told her he was trying not to show how hurt he really was.

"You have to."

"Hey." She gave him a hard squeeze. "You aren't in any condition to argue with me. I am not leaving you, Sawyer Paxton. So be quiet and let's move."

Slade tried to ignore the burning in his side, focusing instead on putting as much distance as they could between themselves and Taras and Javi.

Normally he wouldn't be concerned about Javi. The two had been through enough scrapes together on the inside they could almost consider themselves friends. But he was now certain Javi had told Valeri and the others that he had asked Javi to tell them Clive was dead. It wouldn't come as a surprise. Not now that his cover had been blown. When and by whom were the two questions most prevalent in his mind at the moment.

Information overload, he told himself. Probably didn't help him that one of the bullets had caught him in the side. And the fact that Ashley wouldn't stop trying to examine the wound. Didn't she understand? They didn't have time to stop. Not now. Not yet.

Wherever Valeri was now didn't matter. Slade knew where he'd be at midnight in three days. That was time enough to get Ashley someplace safe and heal up some. Then he'd worry about his next step and finding out what had happened to Georgiana.

He also had to worry about who had sold him out.

That, along with the determined, irritating, kissable blond doctor tucked under his arm, were all that was keeping him going at the moment.

"Okay, we need to stop." Ashley pushed him toward a tree and propped him up as she dropped away. She was breathing heavy, and not, Slade thought, in the way he'd been dreaming about for the past few nights. "We've been walking for—" She lifted her wrist, groaned and took a deep breath. "I really liked that watch. My brother bought it for me for Christmas."

Slade looked down at his right hand. The bleeding had slowed, but it hadn't quit. "Despite the problems it's caused." He leaned his head back, forced his eyes wide to stay awake. He felt as if all his energy had been draining away along with his blood.

"Okay, tough guy. Time to let me take a look." She grabbed the edge of his shirt and tugged it up again. "Any idea where we are?"

"You're trying to distract me while you… Oh, man." The pain surged as she pressed her fingers more firmly against the edges of the wound. "How bad is it?"

"Could be worse." She glanced down at the bag he'd dragged along. "I suppose if there was a flashlight in there you'd have been using it to see where we're going."

He winced. "I have one. I just didn't want to be shining a light around like a beacon with two killers on our trail."

"May I use it now?" She actually batted her lashes at him. It was all Slade could do not to kiss her. The way she could twist that mouth of hers into a lecture without uttering a word was a fine quality all its own.

"Help yourself." He dragged the bag from across his chest and dumped it to the ground.

She crouched, dug for the flashlight, then used it to see what else he'd secreted away. "You've been busy." She pulled out the plastic bag of medications and first aid supplies. He'd also stashed a set of her clothes from her suitcase as well as some of his. "I didn't even notice these things were gone."

"Taras was focused on you stealing stuff, not me."

"Glad I could be of assistance." She angled the flashlight at him and motioned him to get his shirt back up. "Did you grab any gloves?"

"Sorry. Didn't think about it."

"Guess we do this the old-fashioned way, then." She examined the wound more closely this time, making him hiss out through clenched teeth. "You're lucky, *Lucky*. It's a through and through. The bullet missed everything important."

"What else?" Other than it felt like his side was going to ignite into flames.

"You've lost a lot of blood and you're going to lose more traipsing through the forest like this."

She opened a couple of sterile packets of gauze. "I'll get this covered for now. We'll worry about stitching you up once we've got some proper light. I need to find us someplace—"

"We need to."

"Overruled. You'll stay here and wait for me to come back."

"No way!" He was a trained FBI agent. He'd served two tours in Iraq. He did not stay and he certainly didn't wait. He tried to straighten, but became dizzy and, to his mortification, he felt himself tipping forward. She caught him, her hands solidly planted on his chest before he did a face-plant into the dirt.

"Appreciate you proving my point, big guy." She pushed him back against the tree, then guided him to the ground. "Tell me about where we are. Is it popular around here?"

"Not necessarily. It's not vacation time and the cabins in the area are pretty isolated." His stomach pitched. Good thing it was empty.

"Great." She pushed her hair out of her face and turned in a slow circle as he dragged the bag over to pull out a bottle of water. It was a struggle to open the bottle, but he managed and then guzzled the entire contents. "I'll keep going that way," Ashley said, pointing in the direction they'd been headed. "And I'll point the flashlight low to the ground so I don't give away our position. Wow. I sound like I'm stuck in an action movie."

"If you're gone more than thirty minutes, I'm coming after you."

"You try coming after me, you're going to pass out in the shrubs. You stay here, you understand me? I do not want to have to go searching for you."

"I have another solution." The rest had helped clear his head. "Don't come back at all. Keep going."

"I won't do that." There was no hesitation in her voice.

"Why? Because it violates your Hippocratic oath?"

She leaned over and brushed her mouth against his. "Among other things." She cupped his face in her palm, looked into his eyes. "We have unfinished business, remember?"

He laughed. "You cannot honestly be thinking—"

"Will it keep you here?" She tightened her hold on his jaw.

His lips twitched. "Maybe."

"That's enough for me." She got to her feet.

"Ashley, be smart. I'm not worth—"

She glared down at him. Even in the dim light of the flashlight, he saw her eyes flash with temper. "You are worth it to me. Stop playing the martyr and get some rest. I'll be back as soon as I can."

"Wait." He reached into his back pocket and produced the switchblade he'd stolen the day they'd arrived at the cabin. "Take this. Just in case."

She hesitated, but only for a moment. "Back in a bit."

"Yeah," he whispered into the darkness. "I'll be here."

"I knew I should have joined the Girl Scouts." Ashley didn't have a clue what she was doing or where she was going. She had spent her entire professional career in big-city hospitals. Tromping through the forest in the dead of night was the stuff nightmares were made of. Between the wind rustling the trees and the chittering and skittering night creatures, she was really wishing she could pinch herself and wake up.

The few structures she'd passed so far hadn't come close to being habitable, let alone suited to someone with an injury. Her hope was fading fast.

"Maybe we should go back to the cabin," she muttered. She could find a boat somewhere on the lake, couldn't she? No way Valeri and his band of cutthroats would stay there. Not if there was a chance their fears about her watch being tracked were true. As much as she wished Jack would find her, she couldn't help but think the second he did, Sawyer would be returned to prison. She knew one good act, like protecting her, couldn't erase prior bad ones; she could only judge the man she knew, not the one he'd been. At this moment, she deemed him worthy of her help. That was all that mattered.

The outline of a shingled roof in the distance to her left had her pausing in her tracks. It was worth a look. Ashley reached up, grabbed a branch from one of the trees and broke it off. She used it to cut her way through the brush, whacking hard to create a makeshift path she could follow later. The sun began to peek over the horizon, giving her just enough light to see better. She flicked off the flashlight.

She stood in the canopy of the woods, examining the cabin with guarded optimism. It wasn't large. Certainly not in comparison to the palace-like place she'd spent the last few days in. Worn logs and grimy windows told her it had been there for a long while. The tattered clothing hanging from a sagging laundry line indicated possible abandonment. Taking a deep breath, she stepped out from among the trees and headed toward the porch. She knocked on the door, hard, then jumped back and straightened her stretched-out sweater at the neck.

If anyone answered, she'd just say her car had broken down and she was lost. It was pretty close to the truth, anyway. But no one did answer. Ashley jiggled the door handle, felt it give a little. She shoved her weight against the door and pushed. She nearly fell on her face when the door gave way. "Hello?" Ashley called, trying to ease her racing heartbeat. By the time this was over, she'd have her own criminal rap sheet. "Is anyone here?"

Papers shuffled under her feet. She crouched, sifted through the collection of mail that had been stuffed through the slim mail slot in the door. All the dates on the envelopes, mostly overdue bill notices, were years old. Whoever lived here wasn't coming back.

The cabin smelled dank and musty, nothing a few open windows wouldn't cure. She moved through the rooms, tested the faucet in the barely-there kitchen. After a bit of sputtering and straining, the water ran almost clear. A pair of old dusty easy chairs sat in the corner of the main area, a fireplace against the far wall. The bathroom was…interesting, but serviceable.

A bedroom boasted an old, rusted bed still dressed in an aged, dusty quilt. In the closet she found a collection of old clothes hanging on cedar hangers to ward off moths. Oh, yeah. This would work great.

She stripped the bed, flung open the windows. She returned to the bathroom, checked the cabinets but found nothing but linens and towels.

The kitchen cabinets held a collection of canned food and plastic packages all past their best-before date. Under the sink she found a bunch of old grocery bags and a first aid kit, which she tossed on the table to check out later. Before she left, she opened the rest of the windows to air the place out, grabbed the flashlight, then headed back to Sawyer.

She ran this time. The burning in her lungs reminded her she was alive and that she needed to get her butt back to the gym when life righted itself once more. Suddenly, her mundane, work-to-home-to-work life seemed both boring and impossible. So ordinary. But she could seriously do without the constant adrenaline rush she'd been on for... How long had it been?

The more trees she passed, the faster she ran and finally, she recognized the upcoming curve in the path. One turn to the left and...

"Sawyer!" Ashley dropped down beside him. He'd passed out, his hands at his sides, no longer clutching his wound. Now that it was light, she could see more. Blood from the wound had seeped a bit through the gauze, but not badly. "Sawyer? You awake?" She rested her hand on his forehead. He was warm, but not hot.

"Like I could sleep through you touching me. You find something?"

"I did. Here." She dug in his duffel for more aspirin and another bottle of water. "Take these."

He held out his hand and she shook out three pills. He winced when he swallowed.

"You okay to walk?"

"For however long I need to." He pushed himself

up with one hand, far enough she could slip herself back under his arm. "How far?" He leaned on her again and together they got him walking. "Shoot. Bleeding again."

"It's not bad. The sooner we get to the cabin, the sooner I can get you on the road to recovery." What happened after that was an unknown.

"Like Valeri said, pain means I'm alive."

It was slow going, but he seemed to regain some strength as they carefully made their way down the path she'd traveled twice before. Once they reached the cabin, she noticed how he was sucking in air and she felt as if she'd been running for months. He left bloody handprints on the door and frame as she got him inside.

"It's nice. Cozy." Sawyer's voice sounded strained. She saw the color had drained from his face. He was sweating profusely and the cloth she'd given him was bloodied. "Bathroom or bedroom, Dr. Ashley?"

"Bedroom. Better if you lie down. I got the bed ready for you." The air was chilly inside the cabin. She tried to drop him gently onto the mattress, then bent to haul his legs up. "You are a big boy, aren't you?"

"Ow."

"Ow what?"

He looked at her, rolled his eyes. "Besides the hole in my side, there's the gun." He rolled over so she could take the pistol out from the band of his jeans. She set it on the dusty oak nightstand.

"I'll be right back." She headed into the kitchen

to get some water boiling, then realized there was no power. No gas for the stove. No electricity for the small microwave on the counter. "Improvise it is." She went outside and walked around the cabin, found a cord of wood for the fireplace. A few minutes later, she had a fire going and found an old cast-iron Dutch oven in a cabinet.

While the water was coming to a boil, she returned to the bedroom. She found Sawyer sitting up, half-tangled in his shirt. "I was trying to help you," he told her, then seemed to sag in defeat. "I think I'm about out of steam."

"I think so, too." She tugged the shirt over his head, backed up to throw it in the bathroom. She removed the gauze and used a damp cloth to clean the wound. He sucked in a breath. "Sorry. This is going to sting."

"The warning's supposed to come first."

It wasn't her best work, but she managed to get him patched up and, thanks to a tackle box, found a makeshift needle and thread she sterilized in the hot water to stitch him closed. By the time she was done, they were both sweaty, tired and, for want of a better term, cranky.

"Take this." She handed him a glass of water and one of the antibiotics he'd pilfered. "It's the best I can do right now until we get you treated at a hospital."

"That sounds like a rerun." Sawyer choked on the water, but got the pill down. "It's freezing in here." He shivered so hard she thought he'd break.

"I know." And yet, he was burning up. She closed the window, took the quilt outdoors and shook it out. She spotted a collection of old barrels, a worn hose and the old clothesline. She was going to have to rough it for the next little while. Back inside, he was sound asleep, and some of the color was coming back into his face. What she could see of his face.

She sat beside him, the quilt clutched in her lap, and brushed the hair away from his eyes. What did he look like, she wondered, without the beard? That scar. She traced it with her finger. Where had he gotten that scar? And those lips. How she longed to kiss those lips again. To feel his mouth on her own fevered skin.

He was a criminal. A dangerous man, she reminded herself, and yet… Tears burned the back of her throat. And yet, she was falling in love with him.

She swiped a tear from her cheek, shaking her head in disbelief. How her life had changed in such a short time. Once this was all over, once she was back home with her friends, her family, she knew she'd divide her life into two parts. The life she'd had before meeting Sawyer Paxton.

And the life she'd have after.

A life, she forced herself to admit, that could never include him.

Chapter 8

"That should have worked." Eamon sat at his desk and ran the past few hours over and over in his mind. How had Valeri and his group managed to drop completely off the grid? Valeri's entire business was run on technology and internet know-how and yet, even without his main computer go-to, Clive Yblonski, Valeri had managed to simply disappear. Along with Ashley McTavish.

"It did work. Pinging her watch narrowed down the search area." Sarah sat on the edge of his desk.

"To an area already searched." Eamon had been staring at the relevant map. Ashley's watch had gone dead somewhere just outside Lassen National Forest. Unfortunately, none of the roadblocks had reported seeing them, so he was laying odds they'd holed up somewhere. Somewhere planned. Whoever had retrieved the escapees from the bus crash had a destination in mind and they'd probably reached it before this search had been started.

"It's progress. However small," Sarah offered.

"It seems like every time we think we're turning a corner, we end up walking into another brick wall." It wasn't just Ashley's kidnapping or the escape of Marko Valeri. Eamon was encountering this with just about every case he worked. His cell phone buzzed. He checked the screen, saw the text message was from Cole. Frowned. "I've been here too long. I need to get out, clear my head. I'll go on the lunch run. What do you want?"

"Where are you going?"

"The Brass Eagle. Vince's place. Thought I'd try one of his burgers hot this time."

"Sign me up. Let me get my wallet."

"I've got it." He felt bad about keeping her out of the loop, but his instincts told him something wasn't right about this case and his others. "Give me about an hour?"

"Sure. I'll get caught up on the paperwork."

Guilt nibbled at him as he slipped the file Cole requested off his desk and drove down to Vince's bar that doubled as the PI's office. The guilt wasn't so overwhelming that it ate away at his determination, but it was just enough for him to remind himself that he was going to owe his partner, and big, when the time came. He hated lying to anyone, but even now, with everyone's cards on the table, the case was going absolutely nowhere. And it shouldn't be.

When he stepped inside the restaurant, his eyes immediately fell on the two familiar women sitting in a booth by the door.

"Hey, Eamon." Simone Armstrong-Sutton's blue eyes sparkled when she smiled. It made sense they would. The assistant DA hadn't earned the nickname the Avenging Angel for nothing. The prosecutor was known for helping victims find justice across the board and being the one lawyer who defense attorneys hoped they didn't go up against. "How lovely to see you. Kyla and I were just talking about Ashley. Has there been any news?"

"Not yet, no." He was getting weary of uttering those words. "Hi, Kyla."

"Agent Quinn." Kyla nodded.

"It's Eamon, Kyla. You two celebrating?" He looked at the pair of champagne glasses and noted that while Kyla's was just about empty, Simone's was still bubbly and full.

"Kyla's been offered a job with the DA's office." The pride in Simone's voice was clear. "She'll quit being my assistant and become a full-fledged lawyer in the department in a few weeks."

"Just as soon as I find and train my replacement." Kyla finished her drink. "That was the deal."

"It is indeed," Simone said. "Eamon, if there's

anything I can do to help with Ashley, I hope you'll let me know."

"I will. I take it Vince has kept you up to speed?"

"He has. Want to tell me what has you so worried?"

"How do you know I'm worried?"

"You have the same eyes as Chloe." Simone smiled again and tilted her head in a way that had her shoulder-length waves dancing around her shoulders. "She wasn't very good at hiding her feelings, either."

"What a wonderful thing to say to a federal agent." Eamon tried to laugh it off, but even after all these years, the mention of his sister could set his stomach to jolting. He caught sight of Vince at the bar. "If you'll excuse me, ladies. I have an appointment with the owner of the establishment." He stopped long enough to put in his order at the counter, then circled back and headed through the door Vince held open. "Gonna have to make this quick. Cole upstairs in your office?"

"He got here a while ago. Glad you're alone."

"Oh?" Unease pricked at him. "Why?"

"You'll see." Vince led him upstairs to the second floor. The door on the left led to Vince's old apartment, now his brother, Jason's. The door on the right led to home base for Vince's private investigation services.

"He come alone?" Jack asked before the door had closed behind Eamon. Cole was sitting in a chair beside the desk where Jason Sutton was currently focused. He had enough wires and electronics piled around his two computers to open his own RadioShack.

"He did," Eamon said with a bit of bite. "What's all the cloak-and-dagger?"

"We have a bit of a mystery on our hands. That phone that was found on Clive Ybolonski?" Jason poked his head up and turned too-wise eyes on the group. "It's not his."

"Okay." Eamon wasn't sure how that warranted the spy-like text message and expressions of suspicion.

"It's also fingerprint and pass-code protected. Six digits. So far, no luck."

"I find it hard to believe you've called me over here for what you didn't find." Eamon's patience was about to snap.

"I think Jason's hoping we all acknowledge how brilliant he is," Vince said. "Go on, kid."

Jason's mouth twisted wryly, no doubt slightly offended at the nickname despite his almost thirty years. "I dusted for prints first off, but obviously that didn't work. After I struck out with the pass code, I took a trip to the hospital to use Clive's finger. Took a lot of charm, and a little fast-talking, but I've still got some talent in those areas."

Eamon had no doubt. "And?"

"Didn't work." Jason sat back in his chair. "Which didn't make any sense, so I explained about Ashley and asked the nurse to take Clive's fingerprints, brought them back here and compared them to the ones on the phone. They don't match. In fact, none of the prints on the phone belong to Clive."

"Who do they belong to?" Eamon asked.

"That's the question, isn't it? You brought the file?" Jason held out his hand and Eamon passed it over. A few seconds later, Jason made the comparison and nodded. "The prints all belong to one person. Agent Slade Palmer."

"Palmer must have put the phone in Clive's jumpsuit for us to find," Eamon said. "To pass a message?"

"One would assume. There's no telling what his pass code is." Vince frowned.

"And we can't get his fingerprints."

"Sure we can." Jason gave a quick grin. "I have an idea."

"That's not always a good thing," Vince said. "Hack at it, kid."

"On it."

Eamon's frustration was spiking again. "What's he going to—"

"Best you don't ask," Cole suggested. "Just go with it."

"We've got something else." Jack waved them over to the other desk. "Vince did some digging on our prison guards."

"Baxter gave you their names?" Now, that surprised Eamon.

"Hardly. In fact he hasn't been returning my calls

so I went about it in my own special way. Came up with not two, not three, but at least six employees of the prison who have seen a significant jump in income since Valeri arrived on the cellblock. It's sporadic, and different amounts each time, but there's a good-enough pattern to pick up. And, they're all being paid out of the same shell corporation." Jack handed the list over. "A corporation that, once you follow the crumbs, is a subsidiary of one of Valeri's laundering operations. Here's the kicker." Jack's voice hardened. "None of this was difficult to find."

Eamon's heart stuttered before it kicked into overdrive.

"Sorry to say it," Jack added, "but it looks like someone close to this case is keeping information out of the official report. And seeing as it's an FBI operation…"

Eamon sighed, skimmed through the papers. "Either Baxter's holding out on us or he doesn't know there are more guards on the take." Eamon paused. "Or—"

"Or Slade isn't the one who's turned," Cole finished for him.

"What can you tell me about Slade?" Eamon asked.

"Parents died in a car accident when he was seventeen. He joined the army, served six years, honorably discharged with significant commendations. Passed the academy entrance exams and training with flying colors. Spotless record. An impressive one, too. He's gone deep undercover into some pretty bad places. Appears to be a loner, but has a reputation as a straight shooter. Only living relatives are an aunt and cousin. Georgiana Scarpella is the cousin." Vince retrieved another file. "She went missing about two years ago while on vacation with her college roommate. Last reported seen at a club called Kulka in New York. Kulka's on the FBI watch list for ties to suspected human trafficking. Club's run by Edik Valeri."

"Marko Valeri's older brother. Okay." Eamon pinched the bridge of his nose. "That gives us a good idea as to Slade's motivation for getting involved in the Valeri case." Going undercover when the case was that personal was asking for trouble. Eamon knew how hard he pushed when cases hit close to home. He could only imagine the chances Slade was willing to take to find his cousin.

"I also did a little check on Baxter as well as his backup group," Vince said. "Along with yours."

"Sarah?" Eamon shook his head. "No way she's dirty. I'd know."

"You're right. She's clean," Vince confirmed. "Other than a chunk of student debt and an on-again, off-again girlfriend from college—"

"Camille," Eamon supplied. He and his partner were pretty tight.

"Wait, why are we even looking at—"

"Flynn was awfully quick to throw Palmer under

the proverbial bus. Robeson didn't exactly disagree. You don't think that's strange?" Vince asked.

"There hasn't been much about this case that isn't strange." And things were getting stranger by the minute.

"We could start to unravel the strange," Vince said. "If we had some phone numbers to work with."

"You mean Flynn's and Robeson's?" Eamon was staring straight at the line he wasn't sure he could cross. "No. That's taking things too far. Besides, if you're right, if they are involved with Valeri, they wouldn't use agency phones to reach out."

"Doesn't mean they won't get careless if things go off the rails." Vince kept his eyes on Eamon. "If we're wrong, we're wrong. No harm done. But if we're right—"

"If we're right, it's just a matter of time before Palmer's cover is blown," Jack said. "If it hasn't been already."

Eamon shook his head. "I need to think about this."

"Think fast," Cole said. "Jason, you done over there?"

Jason nodded and caught a piece of transparent plastic coming out of the printer. He held it up to the light. "Now, that's a nice thumbprint, Agent Slade Palmer. Let's see if this works." Eamon and the others circled the desk and watched as Jason placed the plastic between the phone and his thumb, keeping the reconstituted print in place. "Got it!

Man, the things you can do with a computer and printer these days."

Eamon's lips flickered. Jason Sutton had served nearly a full stint in prison for his part in a robbery, but when he'd been released, he'd turned his life around, working with and for his brother. Now it seemed as if he was putting his less than admirable talents to good use.

"Okay, let's see what we have here." Jason made room on the desk and put the phone where they could all see it. "Nothing in the call log. The phone's pristine. No apps installed. Just the typical stuff. Let's check the… There we are. Notes. It's just a string of numbers."

"Phone numbers?" Jack asked.

"Too short," Eamon said. "And that's not an area code that exists as far as I know. IP address maybe?"

"Maybe." Jason typed them into the search engine on his laptop. "I don't think Palmer would have made his final message lead us to a florist. Other suggestions?"

"Wait a minute." Cole grabbed a piece of paper, wrote out the numbers, then added periods. "Try this."

"Coordinates?" Eamon asked but even as he did, he knew Cole was right.

"The port of West Sacramento," Jason said and turned his laptop to face them. "Northern California waterways. Helpful for a possible human trafficker."

"That's how Valeri's getting out of the area,"

Eamon said with confidence. Finally, they had a real lead. "We know where he'll be."

"We know the where, but not the when," Jack said. "Jason—"

"Way ahead of you." Jason got busy scrolling through Palmer's phone.

"Doesn't matter when—we'll stake it out," Eamon said. "I need to call…" He looked at his phone, then realized what this entire conversation meant. "I can't call Baxter. Can I?"

"Not until we know for sure if he and his team are in the clear," Vince said. "Between the four of us, we can stake out the port. In the meantime—" he directed a sharp, honed gaze at Eamon "—get finished thinking."

Chapter 9

All that was missing from the idyllic scene, Slade thought when he pried open his eyes, was a pair of cute critters chattering away on the windowsill. A gentle breeze billowed in through the open window, along with thick streams of sunlight that had him wincing. He blinked and groaned, and pushed himself up on one arm. Was there any part of his body that didn't ache? His skin was clammy and his mouth was as dry as worn parchment. His head pounded like a construction crew had taken up residence.

He dragged his feet over the edge of the bed and sat up, wincing as the stitches in his side stretched and strained. Aspirin wasn't going to put a dent in the throbbing or the burning that had at least dropped to a slow flicker. He leaned his head into his hands, took deep breaths until he could move more easily. Rising to his feet, he felt as if he'd crested Mount Everest.

The sunlight coming through the open window seemed cruel and it was all he could do not to stomp over and jam the curtains closed. He made a good attempt, taking short, deliberate steps to the window, but the second he reached the fresh air and the sunshine beat down on him, he stopped. Straightened. And stared at a sight that made the aches and pains vanish in a glance.

Ashley McTavish, hair damp and hanging free against the too-large T-shirt covering her curvy figure, had her arms in a barrel of sudsy water, scrubbing against a washboard that looked as if it had come via a covered wagon decades before. A taut clothesline was strung from the corner of the house to a tree, with sheets, towels, her jeans and sweater all billowing in the breeze.

He smiled, listening to her hum so far off-key he couldn't tell what the song might be, but the enthusiasm and bright shine on her cheeks had him stepping out of the darkness. He'd inhabited that space for almost two years. Too long, he realized. Despite the pain in his body, despite the danger still haunting them, he was grateful to have lived this long and had this one perfect oasis of a moment.

But a moment was all he gave himself. He'd lost

track of their location the second they'd emerged from the lake. All he knew was he'd kept pushing. He glanced down, pressed a hand against the securely taped gauze. She'd stitched him up like the pro she was, making use of the meager supplies he'd been clever enough to pack. He needed to get his bearings. He needed to make a plan. Because Valeri was not going to simply let the two of them get away. Ego, if not self-preservation, would not allow it.

Meanwhile, hiking through the forest without any guidance was only going to get himself and the doctor into more trouble. They had to figure this out. Fast.

After all, he needed to get Ashley home.

And then he needed to finish his job.

Determination swept away the nausea and weakness and he made his way into the bathroom to clean himself up. He pried the bandage off and stripped. The water, once it ran clear, was enjoyably refreshing. He stood there, under the spray, and let his mind wander.

He might have dozed off had Ashley not ripped aside the shower curtain. "What do you think you're doing?" she exclaimed.

He couldn't stop the grin from forming. The T-shirt of his she'd chosen to wear brushed her thighs, and only now did he notice she was wearing the shorts he'd pilfered from her bag. Dr. Ashley had legs. Endless, gorgeous legs, he thought. "You could join me and find out."

"You shouldn't be getting your stitches wet." She turned off the shower and tossed a towel at him. She surprised him again by stepping into the tub and pressing those amazing fingers of hers against the closed wound, presumably to test it. "You should be in bed."

"If you say so."

"We don't have supplies to waste." She gave a good yank on what was left of the bandage, and made him wince. "Next time check with me first."

"Water helps me think." Growing up, whenever he'd had a problem to solve or a hurdle to jump, he'd go swimming or take a shower. The refreshing quality of the water and the calm, steady rhythms of it always helped him see things more clearly. It was one of the reasons he'd joined swim teams in school. Who knew the training he'd gotten there would one day help save his life? Her fingers skimmed over his hip, around to his back, playing against the droplets. "You going to keep exploring down there, Doc?"

She hissed out a breath. "Feeling better, I guess?"

"I've been worse." The lie had her arching her brow when she paused where she was looking.

"So I see."

He'd wondered what her reaction would be to the other scars he'd racked up during his years spent undercover. Would she be quite so fascinated if she had any idea how he'd gotten most of them? He should have known by now that very little scared Dr. Ashley McTavish.

She drew her hand across his chest to the thin, jagged line that had nearly ended him. "What happened here?"

"Someone wanted my dessert." He caught her hand in his, lifted it to his lips and kissed her fingers. "I don't like to share." He grinned.

Her eyes glistened. "Sawyer." The whisper settled around him like a warm blanket. *Don't call me that*, he wanted to say. *My name is Slade. Slade Palmer. And I'm not who you think I am.* But his years of training, years of dedication, kicked in. As much as he wanted to tell her the truth, he wouldn't—he couldn't—go against his instincts and everything he'd learned. It was a long shot, but if she didn't know his real identity and what he was up to, maybe she'd be spared somehow. Man, how he wished that were true.

He kissed her then. A hot, deep, soul-touching kiss that left her gasping, sputtering and smiling.

"We can't," she murmured when she broke free of him. "Not now. You're hurt."

"Not that hurt." He could ignore a lot of the pain if it meant making love to her.

She caught his face in her hands. "You're hurt. And even with my superior repair skills, let's give you a little time to heal, at least."

"We don't have much time." Need slammed through him. To be with this woman. To love this woman before he lost the chance.

"We have enough," she whispered, and kissed

him again. A soft brush of lips. A promise. "I'll find you a change of clothes. Get dressed and I'll fix your bandages."

He chalked up his inability to stop her to his injury, which only now began to throb. But that wasn't his main problem at the moment. She returned seconds later and set the clothes on the counter. When she closed the door behind her, he took a deep, steadying breath.

Then slammed the water on and all the way over to cold.

During the hours Sawyer had slept, Ashley had distracted herself by cleaning, organizing and taking inventory of the supplies in the cabin. Whoever had lived here prior to their arrival had definitely had an interesting mindset. In the closet by the front door she'd found a collection of rolled-up maps and shooting targets, most filled with holes. She did not, however, find any weapons.

She unpacked the duffel bag that had been filled with everything from first aid supplies to packaged snacks, bottles of water and extra clothing. Along with the knife he'd given her and the flashlight, she'd found rope, duct tape—because who goes anywhere without duct tape?—and extra batteries for the flashlight along with a pair of mismatched candles, matches, toiletries and a small wad of cash.

The fire continued to burn, but they were going to need more wood for it soon. There was a generator at the back of the house, but near as she could tell there wasn't any fuel, so…

Thankfully she'd found a can opener in one of the kitchen drawers. They wouldn't starve. Yet. She'd already boiled water and set some in a pot on the stove for drinking. With the fresh air, the cabin was almost…cozy.

She sank into one of the kitchen chairs, careful to avoid splinters, blinking away the exhaustion that began to creep over her. She had no idea what time it was, only that she hadn't stopped until now. Which was probably a mistake.

She couldn't let herself sleep. Not while he did. Not while she was afraid they'd be set upon by Taras and Javi. She jumped at the sound of shifting logs and nearly bolted out of the chair when she found Sawyer sitting on the edge of the hearth, dousing the fire with water. "What are you doing? We need that fire."

"Smoke." He pointed up the chimney, the forced calm on his face telling her she'd made a terrible mistake. "They may be looking for smoke."

"After all this time?" She sank down beside him, watching the last embers burn out. "Considering they have somewhere to be, they can't spend too much time looking for us."

"Don't underestimate them."

"Well, it's been burning a while and we don't have any visitors." Even as she argued, panic surged, along with that hollow feeling at the thought of real life intruding. As much as she wanted to get home, as much as she wanted to let her brother know she was okay, she couldn't help but want to be with Sawyer, which would be impossible once this was all over.

They sat in silence for a while, him staring at the dying fire, her staring at him. Everything seemed caught in a downward spiral, leaving her questioning what would happen next, especially to her, considering her continuing and growing attraction to him.

She longed to kiss him like he'd kissed her in the shower. A kiss she'd struggled to end.

He shifted as if looking to make himself more comfortable.

"You must be hungry." She got to her feet and went over to the cabinets. "We have an interesting selection. There's a lot of baked beans. We can eat those without heating them up, although we probably should. There's canned meat but the dates look a bit iffy." She felt him walk up behind her, stiffened when he laid his hands on her shoulders.

"Ashley."

"You need to eat something." She stood at the sink, staring out the window at the laundry she'd washed earlier. Everything was so oddly simple here. So…quiet and perfect and wrong. "To keep your strength up."

"So do you. Have you slept?"

She shook her head. "No. Not tired."

"Have I mentioned you're a terrible liar?"

"I know." She laughed and found herself leaning back against him. Why would her heart do this to her? Twist itself into knots at the very thought of him. Of a man who was so dangerous and stood in opposition to everything she was. Everything she believed. "Jack says I have a tell, but he won't be specific." She turned to face him. "Do you know what it is?"

"I might." He settled his arms around her, linked his hands behind her back. "How about we save that conversation for another time?" He leaned down, brushed his lips across her forehead. "You should get some sleep."

"I have to patch you up again." She drew him over to the table, where she'd set out a new square of gauze and tape. "The stitches looked okay. They're holding."

"They are."

"Great. So, yeah, just stand right here." She splayed her hands across his stomach, angled him. "Oh. You need to lift your shirt."

"I should have waited to put it on." He dragged the T-shirt up and set her cheeks to flaming. It astonished her just how well-built the man was. Her reaction to him unsettled her. She was a doctor, for heaven's sake. She was well acquainted with the human body. She'd seen her fair share of beautifully maintained ones. But no one, not even her ex, set her blood to singing like this man did.

"All right." She smoothed the tape down with her fingers and sat back. "You're good to go for a bit. Are you sure you're feeling all right? You had a fever—"

"I heal quickly. And I don't stay sick for long." He lowered the shirt, drew her to her feet. "Now you can get some sleep."

She shook her head. "I don't want to." She leaned her head on his chest and squeezed her eyes shut. He smelled amazing. Clean. Hot. Male. He was every temptation she'd ever dreamed of. "I'm afraid if I do, you'll be gone when I wake up." When he didn't respond, she lifted her chin to look at him. His expression said so much and yet nothing at all. "Are you going to leave me, Sawyer?"

He looked over her head, into the thicket of trees on the other side of the yard. "You should leave me. Head for safety as fast as you can. I can't go anywhere. Not while Taras and Javi are out there."

The request that had been on her lips from the moment they met finally pushed free. "There's nothing stopping you from telling me everything now that we're alone."

His body tensed, but he didn't release her. "What do you need to know?"

"Back at the lake when you said *he knew*. What does he know?" She reached up, brushed her fingers against his cheek.

His ocean-blue eyes bored into her, searching, contemplating. "It's best you don't know."

"Best for whom? Please tell me, Sawyer." She needed to understand how, understand why, she could be falling in love with a man like him. A man destined to spend his life either on the run or in prison. "If you can't tell me that, tell me something else. Something about you. Where did you grow up?"

"Ashley—"

"I'm only good enough to want to sleep with, then?"

"That's not true and you know it."

She did know it. She also suspected the accusation would hit its target. Despite his past, she'd gotten a read on him the past few days. He was, with her at least, for want of a better term, honorable. And there was almost nothing sexier and appealing than a man of honor. Even a tarnished one. "Tell me one thing. Just one." She followed him as he circled the kitchen, looking stressed, which seemed odd. "You know I'm a doctor. You know I have a brother. You know I have a tattoo. Oh, wait, no, you don't know that yet, do you?"

His lips twitched. "These last few days have not been brought to you by some matchmaking do-gooder."

"Oh, I don't know about that." How she loved teasing him. "Seems like I found the right guy at the right time to me." She cornered him against the cabinet, feeling success within her grasp. "One thing, Sawyer. Where are you from originally?"

"A little town in Nebraska I'm sure you've never heard of."

He said it so easily, she had no doubt it was true. "Nebraska. Huh. I've never been. Is it nice?"

"It's…" He shrugged. "Sure. Now, how about you do something for me?" He caught her shoulders and gently squeezed. "How about you get some sleep?"

"No."

"Will you if I promise I won't leave?"

"That depends." She narrowed her eyes, tucked her hair behind her ear. "Do you always make good on a promise?"

"Yes, ma'am." Did he have to sound as appealing as he looked?

"Okay." She took a deep breath and released it. "Okay, if you promise, then I'll believe you." She stepped away, walked backward toward the bedroom. "Because the one thing you've never done is lie to me." She only hoped he wasn't starting now.

It was difficult to admit, but watching Ashley disappear down the short hallway to the bedroom made Slade realize he'd rather face ten Valeris than ever betray Ashley.

Lies of omission were one thing. But flat-out, bold-faced lies? She was right. He hadn't uttered one of those to her. Not yet. The Nebraska tidbit had been the first truth about himself he'd uttered in months, years even. It was like reconnecting to a memory long forgotten.

Feeling cooped up, Slade walked outside, circled around to where Ashley had tended to the laundry. He froze, taken aback by the small lake that stretched into the distance. The property was overgrown with trees and shrubs; it obviously hadn't been tended to in ages, but he could tell that at one time, this place had been a perfect hideaway for someone. Would hopefully be the perfect hideaway until Slade could figure out where he went from here.

Slade dragged an old Adirondack chair from where it sat wedged against the back of the house, welcoming the stab of pain and resulting throbbing as he settled in. His stomach growled, reminding himself Ashley had been right when she'd urged him to eat. The idea of food simply didn't appeal. Right now, all he needed was the sunshine, the open lake and endless, abundant fresh air.

He thirsted for the fresh air these days. All those months, those years, locked down behind cement walls and fence had begun to eat away at him in ways he'd never anticipated. Ways he hadn't realized until the night he'd stepped off that bus after the crash. He'd been so determined to learn about Valeri's organization that he'd ignored the warnings and advice of his fellow agents and even the head of his department. Don't do it, they'd told him after

he'd approached Agent Clay Baxter with his idea.
Undercover was one thing.

Deep undercover where you literally had to forget all you were for an unknown amount of time
was quite another. Until the crash, he'd brushed
away the caution. He'd been almost happy to lose
himself in someone else, a fictional someone else
who existed only on paper. The idea of finding
Georgiana had kept him focused. A focus that
hadn't shifted one iota until he'd come face-to-face
with Dr. Ashley McTavish.

She trusted him. No doubt the same way Georgiana trusted Slade would save her. That was the
fear that triggered his nightmares. That his cousin
woke up every day wondering where he was. Why
hadn't he found her, she probably asked herself? Or
worse, what if she believed he'd stopped looking?

Slade pushed the fear into the space he'd kept
locked for years. He got to his feet, embracing the
ache in his side, and returned to exploring the cabin
and surrounding area. Nothing surprising. Nothing
out of place or out of the ordinary. There was a root
cellar that had nothing more than a collection of
crates that might have held canned or jarred goods
once. He also found two empty fuel containers that
he brought outside with him on the off chance that
inspiration would strike and he'd locate some gas
for the generator.

Inside the house, he investigated the cabinets,
agreed with Ashley that the cans of beans were

probably their best bet for sustenance once their protein bars ran out. The appliances were modern, but not particularly contemporary. He wandered down the hall, poked his head in and found Ashley sound asleep in the same spot he'd occupied earlier. Her hair lifted against the breeze in a way that had him fighting temptation to do as she'd urged earlier and join her in that bed.

He ignored the unfamiliar twisting in his chest and left, closing the bedroom door behind him. In the hallway, he returned his attention to the bathroom, looked out the small round window. The house seemed larger from the outside. Slade went back outdoors, examined the bathroom side of the cabin this time and, when he reached the end of the structure, glanced behind him at the window. He pressed his hands flat against the side of the house, measured at least a good ten to twelve feet of extra space that wasn't part of the bathroom. He looked up and found two sets of air vents along the sloped roofline. "I should have thought of it sooner—"

Back in the cabin, he examined the linen closet next to the bathroom. The space was barely deeper than a bookcase. He removed the few contents, mostly old, worn towels and bedding, then the shelves. Once he could wedge himself inside, he looked for a trigger lock, a button, something. He found nothing.

He was sweating again, feeling nauseated, and took a break to grab a protein bar and water. Sitting on one of the chairs, he stared down the hall at the closet. Looked down at the floor. He pressed his foot hard against the boards. Solid. At least where he was sitting. A few minutes later, he confirmed the rest of the flooring was securely in place. No creaks. No odd separations. No trapdoors.

Flashlight in hand, he returned to the linen closet, and saw faint scratch marks arcing out from the corner along the floorboards. He felt around the edges of the doorframe. There. Under his right hand about midway down. A latch. He flicked it open, dug his fingers in and pulled.

The rear wall of the closet opened like a door. As Slade stepped inside, he aimed the light up and around. Metal bunk beds. A desk piled with books and papers, and on the wall above them a corkboard was stuffed with images, maps and notes. The worn, scarred table to his right held a hot plate and nearby a couple of dishes, an old pot and a pan. More canned food, packaged meals. Bottled water.

A beat-up locker sat beside the entry to the room. He lifted the latch and found a handgun, two hunting rifles along with a shotgun. Relief swept over him. He gathered up the weapons, took them into the kitchen, then returned for the boxes of ammunition that had been neatly arranged on the shelf above.

A plan began to form. Rough. Ragged. Needing details and help, but he'd work it out as the day progressed.

He pulled down the papers above the desk, rolled them up and carried them out with him.

Once the room was hidden once more, he checked and loaded the weapons, then left them by the front door, keeping the handgun on the table beside him.

Slade unrolled the map, recognizing the general area as where they'd been living for the past few days. Not that the former occupant of the cabin had been good enough to mark their exact location. That would have been too easy. Other markings, however, could indicate other cabins in the area. If nothing else, he had his bearings.

Now all he needed for his plan was the strength and courage to see it through.

Chapter 10

"That's it." Sawyer's voice brushed against her ear, his arms encircling her as he readjusted her grip. She braced her feet apart, her center of balance only slightly wobbly as his body pressed against her back. "Look down the sight. Close your less dominant eye if you have to and...squeeze."

"What about the noise? You were concerned about the smoke from the fire. Won't Valeri—"

"I'm more concerned that you know how to protect yourself. Besides, I'm back on my feet. I can handle what's coming."

Sure, he could. But could she? She pulled the trigger. The empty bean can resting on the fence post shot into the air and disappeared into the bushes. The blast echoed up and into the trees. Ashley looked over her shoulder in time to see the surprise jump into his eyes. "Not too bad, huh?"

"Not bad at all." He took hold of her shoulders and pivoted her to the right. "Let's try—"

Ashley aimed again, fired off five more consecutive shots and sent the next five targets flying. Then she put the last four bullets in the clip into the scarred tree ten feet beyond the fence in a tight ring. She released the clip, let it drop into her hand, and set both it and the nine millimeter onto the picnic table beside them. "Want me to reload?"

"I guess I should have asked if you could shoot." He stepped away and scrubbed a hand across the back of his neck. "I thought you said you don't like guns."

"Doesn't mean I can't use one." Because she felt the need to keep her hands busy, she went ahead and reloaded the clip. "My ex-husband had a collection of them. No way was I going to live in a house with them without knowing how to use one safely and correctly. Which means…" She changed her mind. So first she clicked the safety, then set the weapon and the clip down on the picnic table. "We've officially come to the get-to-know-you portion of our time together. I've been married before. How about you?" She folded her arms over her chest.

"How about me what?" He still looked a bit dazed, which did her ego a bit of good.

"Have you been married?" She reached for one

of the water bottles and drank, keeping her eyes on him.

"No. Too busy."

"Right." And just like that, her flirty mood faded. She swallowed hard, trying to appreciate his constant reminders he was not someone to get involved with. "How about—"

"Ashley."

She shook her head, turned her attention to the lake and moved toward the shoreline. "How about I tell you all about my ex-husband and you can tell me who you really are. Seems like an even trade of information to me."

"Ashley, stop."

He moved toward her, was inches away from touching her again, but she stepped away, hating herself for wanting him. Berating herself for not being able to conquer these impossible, confounding feelings she had for him. Her empty stomach rumbled. "Do you think there's fish in that lake?"

"What?" He followed her gaze. "Uh, probably. Did your ex-husband teach you to fish, too?"

"My dad and brother. I was a bit of a tagalong. Whatever Jack was doing, I wanted to do. I think we should try to catch something to eat."

"All right. I saw some fishing gear—" He moved past her, but she reached out and grabbed his arm, moved in front of him.

"Who are you?" She stared up at him, confusion and doubt circling inside her like a restless shark ready to chomp down on its prey. "How is it you are the way you are with me but...?" Words failed her.

"Maybe you just bring out a different side of me." His smile didn't quite reach his eyes. "It's all right, Ashley. I understand." He brushed a finger down the side of her face.

"How can you when I don't? It's like you're two different people, but neither one has done anything other than protect me." Her voice lowered to a whisper, as if she were uttering a prayer. "How can I want to be with you when I know what you've done?"

He shook his head, slipped his hand around to the back of her neck, his fingers massaging her tense muscles. "I don't have an answer for you, Ashley. I can only tell you what you're feeling isn't one-sided. I want you, too."

"But there's nothing beyond this, is there?" The longing she'd once buried surged. She was a good doctor. She made a difference. There shouldn't be this empty space inside of her, the space that had cratered open when her marriage had fallen apart. When she'd realized the home and family she'd thought would be hers had never been within her grasp. And now, she was with a man who she hadn't even known until a few days ago and didn't want to walk away from without having known what it was like to lie in his arms. "This time, here, it's all we're going to have, isn't it?"

"I think we both know this isn't going to end well

for me." His lips curved before he brushed his mouth against hers. "All the more reason you should leave me. Now. I can get you away. Before they find us."

"I don't want to leave you." She lifted up on her toes to kiss him. "Ever."

"That's not reality, Ashley." He smoothed his other hand down her hair. "The reality is you have a life to go back to. You have a career and your friends and family. And that reality is closing in on us. There's nothing either of us can do to stop it. We can only try to deal with it."

Something in the way he spoke, in the words he chose, sent a new shiver running down her spine. "You have a plan." She peered into his eyes, looking for hints of the truth. A truth he still hadn't completely confessed to her. She could see it, hovering behind the curtain he kept draped over his heart. "What are you—"

"Not now. Please." He drew her against him, buried his face in her hair. "I don't want to talk about it or even think about it, I want to be with you, Ashley, for as long as I can. But I'll understand if you can't—"

She slipped her mouth over his, stopping whatever else he was going to say. Drawing his doubts, his fears, his longing, into her as she breathed him in. When she felt certain he'd gotten her answer, she lifted her mouth just enough to whisper, "Be with me, Sawyer. Be with me now." She moved her hands down his arms, slid her fingers through his. Together they walked back into the house.

The incongruity of Sawyer Paxton did not slip from Ashley's mind as she led him inside to the bedroom. But nothing could change the fact that her heart at this moment beat only for him. The sun's rays filtered through the open window, the cool breeze dancing across her skin as lightly as Sawyer's fingers skimmed down her arm.

"I'll be right back."

She stood beside the bed, looking between the empty doorway and the rumpled sheets. Nerves she hadn't known she possessed skittered to life. She was at a crossroads, she knew. A decision there was no coming back from. A decision she wasn't going to take back. If this was all she could have, these stolen moments with him, moments that would only be between the two of them, she'd take them. She'd take him.

When he returned, it was with the foil packets that she recognized from her medical bag back at the cabin. She looked at them when he set them on the nightstand, then quirked an eyebrow in his direction. "Pretty sure of yourself, were you?"

"Hopeful." He reached for her, but instead of wrapping her in his arms, he slipped his hands beneath the edge of her shirt and drew it over her head, tossing it to the floor. "I'd like to thank the doctor for making sure her bag was properly supplied. I've been dreaming of this almost from the moment I first saw you."

"Almost?" She teased as his hands smoothed their way up her sides, cupped her breasts through her white cotton bra. Ashley took a deep breath and tried to calm her spiraling emotions. Her nipples peaked, strained beneath his tortuous touch.

She wanted—no, she needed—to touch him. Her restless hands moved up, then down his arms, gripped the fabric of his shirt into her tight fists. "Off," she gasped as he lowered his mouth to the side of her neck and kissed her. "I want this off. I want to feel you. All of you." Together they pulled his shirt free and sent it soaring to join hers.

"Now this." Sawyer's voice rumbled, setting her pulse to racing. His fingers made quick work of the clasp at her back, releasing her bra. He slipped the straps down her arms in such a slow, sensuous trail her knees nearly buckled. He bent as he removed her bra, placed his mouth in the valley between her breasts, and cupping one in his palm, kissed the tip.

Ashley threaded her hands through his thick hair as she rode the sense of pleasure coursing through her body. She rocked against him, whimpering as he gave the same attention to her other breast, drawing it into his mouth and caressing with his tongue.

"Sawyer." His name was a whispered plea as his fingers slipped beneath the waistband of her shorts. She held her breath as he eased the fabric over her hips. When he placed his open mouth against her navel, she groaned, her blood pounding at the promise to come.

He guided her to the bed then, removing the last of her clothing when she lay back. She reached for him, needed to feel his hands on her, but the sight of the bandage cleared the fog in her brain, and as he leaned over, pressed a knee between her thighs, she touched his wound. "Be careful of your stitches."

He froze, arms planted on either side of her shoulders, and looked at her. His long, rich chestnut brown hair draped his face, though it didn't hide his wide smile. She couldn't help it; she had to laugh. "Yes, Doctor." He kissed her so deeply, so soul-searchingly perfect she had to hold on to him to stop from tumbling over the edge. His fingers trailed along the top of her thigh before slipping to her core. She moaned and pulsed beneath his touch. Her hips arched, trying to bring him deeper, even as she tore her mouth free from his.

"Not enough." Her hand fumbled for the button on his jeans. She wanted him, all of him, inside of her.

"Not yet." He pressed kisses to her mouth, her eyelids, her neck, her shoulders, until she forgot her own name. She cried out as the wave began to crest. "Go over, Ashley." His gentle command sliced through her already breaking heart. "Let me see you go over. Let go." He tangled his tongue with hers, pushing the last bit of reason from her mind as the pressure inside her built.

When she did soar over the edge, she opened her eyes, looked into his and the triumph she saw there had her calling his name. The tremors subsided. Her body mellow and sated, she sank into the mattress. As she calmed and caught her breath, he stood up and discarded his jeans. She spotted the barely there wince as he reached for her again.

"No." She planted a hand on his chest and pushed him onto his back with far more agility than she thought she possessed. She had him beneath her, his head cushioned on the pillows as she reached for protection. "This time it's my turn, so you let go." She pushed his mouth open with hers, diving in to explore and tempt and arouse as he had done for her. She felt the hot length of him pulsing close to her heat. Ashley flattened her hands against his torso, sliding them across his taut stomach. He sucked in a breath. His body tightened. The pulse in his neck hammered.

"Ashley." He'd ground out her name. His control had to be slipping.

A wicked grin spread across her mouth and she held the protection up to him. "No teasing allowed."

She sighed and gave him the room he needed to sheathe himself. When he reached for her, she braced her hands on his shoulders, and took him deep inside. Never had she felt this complete before. Sawyer's hands locked around her arms and steadied her as she rocked her hips, the mind-numbing pleasure building quickly inside her once more. He moved under her, his hips matching hers. His groans matching hers. He released her and she peaked and arched, throwing back her head as the climax overtook her, now drawing him over the edge with her.

She fell forward, wanting nothing more than to feel the length of his body beneath hers. Their heartbeats in sync and their breathing ragged. His hands dived into her hair, keeping her close to him even as he shifted them to their sides. She turned her face into his neck, inhaling the scent of him. Memorizing it. Memorizing every part of this moment.

"Are you okay?" she murmured against his skin. "Your wound—"

"I'm fine." He wrapped his arm around her, keeping her where she was as he drew the sheet up and around them both. He pressed a tender kiss against her temple. "We're fine. Get some rest."

"I don't want to rest."

"I want you to rest." He settled his hand on her hair and stroked it. "Because I'm not done with you yet."

Her heart skipped a beat. But a solitary tear slipped free and trailed down her cheek.

Ashley popped part of a protein bar into her luscious mouth. "You do realize that once we finish these treats, we'll be relegated to the coming apocalypse rations in the cupboards."

"I'm feeling a bit adventurous right about now." He handed her back the water. Lounging around in bed with a beautiful woman seemed an appropriate last act. Or close to a last act, Slade thought. He could hear the clock's tick-tick-tick indicating the future coming toward them, but he was determined to enjoy what he could. And seeing Dr. Ashley McTavish free and happy and loving the moment was definitely something he enjoyed. "Speaking of adventures."

"Hmm?" She leaned against the headboard, pulling the sheet just high enough around her to cover her full breasts while she licked crumbs from her fingers. The grin she shot him made him wish he'd stashed more condoms in that escape bag of his. "What's on your mind?"

"Your ex-husband. What happened?"

Her brow furrowed. "You want to talk about Adam? Now?"

He shrugged. "No time like the present. Why'd you break up?"

She swallowed, then drank some water and for the first time since they'd made love, seemed to look anywhere but at him. "Lots of reasons. I had stars in my eyes when I married him. I was just out of med school. He'd just been selected for his first undercover assignment."

Slade's mouth went dry. "He was a cop?"

"Fourth generation. Undercover mostly. Chicago. He came into my ER needing stitches. He flirted. I flirted back. Three months later we got married. My parents were thrilled."

"Were they really?" Slade asked even as his mind spun. She'd been married to a cop. An undercover cop just like him.

Ashley smirked. "No. I mean they supported me. Jack was more vocal about it. Probably because he already knew what I didn't. Being married to a cop is hard enough. Being married to an undercover?" She shook her head. "I admire the people who can do it, but I couldn't. Sometimes I wonder if he hadn't been so honest with me about what he was doing. Maybe then that constant fear, the worry, wouldn't have knotted so tight inside of me. I kept expecting him in my ER. I'd go weeks, sometimes months, without seeing him and then when I did, all this, I don't know, anger would just bubble up and we'd argue. Especially about having kids. I wanted them. He didn't. Not until he was more settled with his career, he said. When the arguments wouldn't stop..." She shrugged. "We made it two, almost three years before I called it quits."

He listened. Absorbed. Accepted. She wasn't telling him anything he hadn't heard from other agents who worked undercover. "That must have been difficult."

"Not after I found out about the pregnant girlfriend." Her smile was quick and didn't come close to reaching her eyes. "That's an effective bucket of ice water on the bloom of romance, let me tell you. Turns out he did want kids. Just not with me."

"Do you still want kids?" The second he asked, he wanted to pull the words back. Why was he letting himself think they might have a shot when this was all over?

"Oh, yeah." She ducked her chin. "I love kids. I always wanted a houseful, even when I decided to go to medical school. Always figured I'd find a way to make it all happen. Be one of those women who had everything they wanted."

"There's still time." It was all Slade could do not to touch her. The last thing he wanted to do was give her hope—false or otherwise. Whatever inkling he might have had about telling her the truth about who—and what—he was vanished under the weight of her confession. He never wanted to be the cause of her fear and worry. He wouldn't put her through that. Not with what he had left to do. "You can still have what you want."

"I'm not sure anymore." She shook her head and finally looked at him. "What about you? How did… all this happen to you?"

"You mean how did I end up serving a life sentence?" He said it out loud as a reminder, not only for her, but for himself. He could feel Sawyer Paxton fading beneath the desires of Slade Palmer. He'd never had a relationship last more than a few months, mostly because he was always on the move with his job. Marriage, a family, love in the long-term, it all needed stability and roots to grow and he barely stayed in one place long enough to coax out a few weeds. He couldn't start wanting those things now, not when his future was so uncertain.

Someone in the agency had betrayed him to Valeri, who was still on the loose, with information Slade needed. That had to come first.

He could, at least, make certain Ashley was safe. Something she wouldn't be until he closed his case.

"Sawyer?" Her fingers brushed lightly over his arm. "Tell me?"

"No." He caught her hand and kissed the tips of her fingers. He couldn't do this. He didn't want to lie to her anymore. "I don't want you to know that part of me. I did what I had to do to survive, Ashley. I did what I needed to—" To what? Get the job done?

"Then how about you tell me about this." With her other hand, she traced the scar on his face. "No more jokes."

"I got careless." He'd made a mistake. Lowered his guard. Forgotten he was without friends inside and he'd paid the price. "In prison, everyone's in a corner. I got in someone's way." And earned a spot on Valeri's crew.

"And this one?" She bent down, pressed her lips against the puckered scar on his shoulder.

"Knifed by a bank robber. Ashley." He leaned over and kissed her before she asked another question. "Stop. Let's just enjoy what time we have."

"Because we're running out of it." She looked him straight in the eye. "Aren't we?"

"We are. I can't stay here. When they come for me—"

"They want me, too. At least, Olena does."

He had to give her credit. The fear barely registered in her voice. "She won't hurt you. I promise you that, Ashley." He kissed her again. Hard. And as long as it took for her resolve to soften. "You have a life, Ashley. I'm nothing more than a blip. Your family and friends need you. Your job needs you. You have lives to save, to change. Which is why, when the time comes, you're going to have to trust me."

"Oh, I am, am I?" She tilted her head, eyes narrowed in challenge.

"You are. Because I can't do what I have to if I'm worried about you. Do you trust me, Ashley?"

She sighed. "Of course I trust you." She pressed her mouth to his. "I love you."

The words struck him silent. He squeezed his eyes shut, pushing the joy those words brought him into the deepest, most protected part of his soul. He couldn't utter the same words that wanted to fly out of his mouth. To do so would only strengthen the tether he felt forming between them. What he felt for Ashley he'd never felt for any woman before. He wouldn't feel it again. Not for as long as he lived. "Then promise me you'll do what I ask. Please, Ashley. Do that for me."

"Sawyer, I—"

"Swear it," he pressed. "Swear it on your brother's life. On Jack's life." Defiance flashed in her eyes and that spark of anger thrilled him like little else had before. She was going to be okay. When all this was over, however it turned out for him, she was going to be okay. Right now, that was all that mattered. "Ashley?"

"I swear it on Jack's life." Her eyes filled with tears. "I'll do it." Her lower lip trembled and he kissed her, his heart breaking all the while.

Special Agent in Charge Don Harrison slid into the booth across from Eamon, gesturing to the waitress for a cup of coffee. He set a thick file folder on the table. "I have to say, Eamon, you always find a way to surprise me. I hope this is as important as you said. Otherwise I'm going to have some serious explaining to do to my daughter for missing her volleyball finals. I'm supposed to be on vacation." He flashed a smile at the waitress. "Thanks."

"Anything else?" the waitress asked.

"No," Eamon said before his boss's boss could respond. He'd gotten used to the eye-watering smell of overgrilled meat and burned onions. Barely. "Maybe later."

"Definitely later," Don said. "Only time I get to eat red meat is when I'm out of Catherine's line of sight. Why does it feel as if I'm in some weird Gothic TV show? All that's missing is cherry pie…"

Don trailed off, his eyes sharpening as they landed on Eamon. "You look awful."

"Makes sense since I feel like it." Eamon glanced out the window toward the setting sun. Four days. They were going on four days since Valeri and his crew had disappeared after the crash. Four days since Ashley had been seen. Four days since Eamon had promised Jack he'd get his sister back to him. "I was called in on the prison bus crash."

"So that's why you had me pull the Valeri file. Any reason you didn't go through Clay Baxter?"

Eamon simply stared.

"All right." Don's eyes sharpened. "We'll come back to that. The escapees took a hostage, didn't they? Local doctor?" He lifted the mug to his lips, took a long drink. "Man, no one does road coffee like a diner in the middle of nowhere."

"Yes to both. Dr. Ashley McTavish." Eamon didn't miss the flinch on Don's face. "She's the sister of a friend."

Don didn't need any further information to understand what Eamon was telling him. "What's got you spooked?"

Eamon had been rehearsing what to say during the entire drive over here. He was running on fumes, but his mind wasn't anywhere close to slowing down. "You didn't tell anyone where you were going, did you?"

"I did not. And I turned off my car's GPS like you asked."

"Good." Eamon had done the same after choosing an out-of-the-way diner a good half hour from Sacramento off I-5. "I left Agent Nelson back in Sacramento. Told her I was following up on one of the financial trials for Valeri's trafficking ring."

"Something the case agents and prosecuting attorneys missed?"

"You could say that."

"And whatever it is you've found you haven't shared with your partner."

"She's new. If this goes bad, I don't want it blowing back on her. I'm old and jaded. I can take it."

"That remains to be seen."

"We have a problem, Don. A big one." Eamon picked up the file he had brought and stashed on the red vinyl seat next to him.

Don sighed. "Always knew my open-door policy with my agents was going to get me in trouble one day." Don Harrison had been ten years in with the FBI when Eamon joined. Don had been his first boss, his mentor, and was, quite possibly, one of the few people in the world Eamon knew would steer him right. "Whatever it is, let's get it on the table. Literally." He glanced down at the file.

"Did you know the case against Marko Valeri is still ongoing?"

Don nodded. "They're trying to use him to get to his brother, who actually runs the operation, both here and overseas. We're about ready to bring in Interpol, but the agency's trying to keep it all quiet, though. Letting everyone think the case closed with Valeri's conviction."

"It didn't work. There's a leak on Baxter's team."

Don was about to take another drink of coffee, but he set his mug down abruptly. "That's a big accusation for a small team, Eamon. Baxter and, what, two others?"

"Three, actually. Agents Caleb Flynn and Tony Robeson."

"Three? Really? Who's the third?"

"Undercover agent. Slade Palmer."

"Palmer?" Don whistled. "So that's what happened to him. Been wondering. Rumor was he burned out and took an extended leave for family issues. You're telling me he's been working with Baxter?"

"You didn't know?" As SAC, Don Harrison should have been aware of any and all investigations in his region.

"I did not. How deep in is he?"

"Palmer's been in Folsom Prison for the past eighteen months in the hopes of getting close to Valeri. This wasn't sanctioned, was it?"

"Not by me." Don pushed his mug aside and tugged the file to him, flipped it open. "Baxter's been playing this pretty close to the vest. Even more than usual. Tell me what else you know."

Eamon spelled it all out, keeping things as detailed as possible but also as concise as he could manage. "Baxter's claiming they haven't heard from Palmer in over a month. Said he's missed his check-ins."

Don shook his head. "Doesn't sound like Slade. Guy is as by the book as it gets. Quantico's been after him to head up a new undercover training program we're trying to get off the ground. He's good, Eamon. As good as they get."

"So if I told you Agent Flynn suggested that Palmer turned and is now working for Valeri, you would say—"

"I'd say Agent Flynn is very confused." Color flushed Don's face. "No way do I believe that. What did Baxter say?"

"Baxter defended Slade. But I could see by the time Flynn was done, Baxter had his doubts."

"What's all this about prison guards?" Don ran his finger down a page in the file.

"We've discovered at least six guards are working for Valeri."

"Six? No, that's not right. The file says…" He pulled over the file he'd brought himself and flipped through pages. "My file says three."

"File's wrong. My source is pretty thorough."

"Your *source*?"

"I don't think you want me to answer that question, sir," Eamon added. "Let's just say he has no vested interest and is even more determined than I am to get Ashley home safely." That was all he cared about. Whatever happened with Valeri, he'd deal with later. "Flynn stated that it was one of his informants that put them on to the fact Valeri was still running his operation from behind bars. I can't look into that without raising any alarms."

"I can do that." Don pulled out his cell and began keying in notes. "What's going on with these guards?"

"The three Baxter told us about or the rest we found out about?"

Don lifted his gaze to Eamon. "You haven't talked to Baxter about this."

"No, sir. I can't. Not until I know where the leak is coming from. It has to be someone close to the investigation. After speaking to the wardens at both Folsom and Pelican Bay, they confirmed the transfer order came through the FBI. That, honestly, doesn't make a lot of sense since Folsom is a state prison. They had help waiting for them when the bus crashed. They had a plan and Valeri's outside communication has been monitored. Or so we've been told."

"What about the crash? Was that part of the plan?"

"Forensics confirm they didn't find any evidence of tampering."

"So you want to look into Baxter's, Robeson's and Flynn's backgrounds."

"Actually, sir, that's already been done." Eamon pulled out the second folder.

"Tell me Baxter came out okay. Otherwise we're

going to have a ton of closed cases that'll be called into question."

"We didn't find anything untoward in his background." Eamon understood his boss's relief. "But we did learn that Flynn's college scholarship was sponsored by a company that was, up until five years ago, connected to one of Edik Valeri's businesses. Flynn's mother was a cousin. She died when Flynn was still in high school. He was taken in by her relatives."

"You're saying this was some kind of quid pro quo? He gets his education and a sweet future, and in return, ends up as a plant in the FBI?"

"Edik and Marko would see it as an investment. In fact, I wouldn't be surprised if Flynn's not the only one in law enforcement with those kinds of connections. We also—"

"Who is this *we*, Eamon?"

"A private citizen who wishes to remain so, sir." No way was Eamon going to out Jason Sutton to one of the big bosses at the FBI. Besides, he didn't think Don would appreciate knowing all this information came courtesy of a one-time felon even if said felon had redeemed himself and was now a law-abiding citizen. "He's backed it up from numerous angles. We have copies of all the documents—"

"Documents that would have required a warrant to obtain."

"I wasn't looking for information for prosecution, Don." He was down the career-ending rabbit hole now. "I'm looking for a way to find my friend's sister. And to save Agent Palmer's cover from being blown."

"Might be too late for that." Don held up a finger when Eamon started to speak. "I need to make a call. Order me a burger. Medium rare. Double order of fries. We're going to be here a while."

To give his boss some privacy, Eamon went to the counter to order and, before he returned to the table, directed his attention to Vince, who was seated at the table closest to the door. Eamon gave a quick nod, earned one in return, and turned away when Vince resumed eating and reading a newspaper.

When he got back to the table, Don was scribbling on the back of one of the file folders. "Got it. Okay. I want you to get me an additional team of agents to Sacramento within the hour…No," Don snapped, "I'll explain when they arrive. Best of the best, Jane. Ones you'd want looking for your family…Uh-huh…Right…Thanks." He clicked off. "First of all, you want to call your buddy over? Might save you time later on if he hears it all directly from me."

Eamon stared.

"I trained you, remember?" Don leaned to his right, waved a hand and, a few moments later, Vince appeared beside the booth. "You would be Eamon's source, I take it?"

"One of them. Vince Sutton." He nodded and joined them in the booth.

"SAC Harrison. We're about to open a whole field of hornets' nests, gentlemen." He sat back as his burger was delivered. "Edik Valeri flew into San Francisco two days ago along with three of his team. A fleet of SUVs picked them up at the airport, then, nothing. We've lost track of them."

"Can't be a coincidence," Eamon said.

"No," Don agreed. "It isn't." He turned his phone around and showed an image with two pictures. "You recognize them?"

Eamon looked closer. "No. Vince?"

Vince shook his head.

"The man is Taras Valeri. Edik's oldest son. Former special forces in the Russian army. He's his father's right hand and chip off the old, evil, rampaging block."

"And the girl?" Eamon asked.

"Olena Podrova. She's Marko's daughter."

Vince whistled low under his breath. "We didn't find any record—"

"You wouldn't have. Her mother's Ukrainian. She was raised on the border and only found out about Valeri a few years ago. Just after she turned thirty."

"Thirty?" Eamon pointed at the image of the girl in a school uniform. "She can't be more than, what, thirteen in that picture?" There was a fresh-faced innocence about her. Round cheeks, long dark hair, a mouth that looked unaccustomed to smiling. But there was no mistaking the eyes. She had her father's vacant eyes.

"It's the most recent photo we could find."

"Meaning we have no idea what she looks like now. Great."

"She's definitely taking after Daddy. She's made a name for herself as a mercenary and changes identities like we change shirts. While we can track Taras's arrival in the States to just after Marko's arrest, we can only rely on official rumors that Olena's here. Interpol has been after her, but the Valeri name, legal or otherwise, offers a lot of protection. We have to assume she's here and helping her father."

"The help Valeri had waiting when the bus crashed," Eamon said. "Could be them."

"Could be," Vince agreed. "What now?"

"I suggest you both get something into your stomachs," Don said. "Because from here on, we're not going to have time to eat."

"Any idea where Edik and the others are headed?" Vince asked.

"No," Don mumbled around a too-full mouth. "None at all."

Vince gave Eamon's boss a chilly smile as the waitress approached. "Then it's a good thing we do."

Chapter 11

It was domestic bliss, in its own way, Ashley thought. In fact, it had her wishing she and Sawyer could hole up in this cabin forever. But she was, after all, a practical and realistic woman. She knew the bubble she'd inhabited alone with Sawyer was going to pop. She also knew that when it did, she'd likely never be the same.

He'd left the bed while she slept and when she awoke, the loneliness and longing had dropped over her like a heavy weight. It had her out of bed and dragging on her discarded clothes.

She padded barefoot through the cabin, unease pricking through her when she realized she was on her own. She returned to the bedroom and leaned out the open window, but other than the remnants of her laundry only the lake and chairs greeted her.

Whatever time she had with Sawyer was ticking away and fast. She'd thought she understood what dread felt like waiting for Adam to come home, wondering if he was wounded or... Ashley shook her head to dislodge the thought. She didn't have the first clue what real fear was then, she realized.

Nor did she have any concept of what real love was. What she felt for Sawyer, when she looked at him, when she felt his arms around her, when he whispered in her ear and refused to make promises he knew he couldn't keep, that was what would warm her on the hard nights ahead.

Her love for Sawyer—what did that say about her? Was there something wrong with her? Or had she simply fallen in love with a man who had made terrible, horrible mistakes? She would have, she knew, many, many hours to think on that.

She left not just the bedroom, but the cabin and caught sight of Sawyer crouched in front of the line of trees outlining the property. It was a beautiful spot. She looked up through the treetops into the crystalline blue sky and the errant, puffy clouds passing by. The air invigorated her.

Ashley walked toward him, a frown forming as she watched him line up small sticks and thin branches before covering them with leaves. "What are you doing?"

He glanced over at her, down at her bare feet.

"Setting up a warning system. You should be wearing shoes."

She should be wearing… Sometimes his concern for her robbed her of her senses. "What kind of warning system? You don't really think Taras's going to find us? Out of all the cabins, in all of the forest—"

"He'll find us." He reached for another stack of twigs, then pulled a rifle off the ground. "I'm going to make sure of it."

"What?" She started forward, stepped on a sharp rock, and stopped, pressing her lips tight against the pain. Ashley shifted positions. She wasn't in the mood to hear an *I told you so.* "What do you mean you're going to make sure he finds us?"

"I need him to. He's my only way to Valeri."

"Valeri's gone."

"Not entirely, I hope." He set another batch of branches beneath leaves, this one in another slight clearing before he gathered more and continued on around the house.

"Aren't you going to turn yourself in?"

"No." He took her arm, steered her back into the cabin. "Let me see your foot."

"My foot's fine." He'd seen that? He really didn't miss a trick.

"You cut it on a rock out there. Let's see it." Sawyer gestured to a kitchen chair.

"I'm the one who should be checking your

wound," she grumbled. "I am, after all, the doctor in the house."

"My wound is fine. I think you've tended it just perfectly. And frequently." He bent down, lifted her leg and cradled her calf in his hands. "Looks like it hurt."

She shrugged.

"Let me guess. You're not one who likes to hear *I told you so.*" He retrieved the first aid kit.

She refused to give him the satisfaction and remained silent. "If you turn yourself in, we could still see each other. You know, once they let you have visitors again."

His hand stilled from where he was swabbing alcohol over the wound. "Ashley—"

"I know it's not a perfect solution, but I can't just say goodbye and never see you again."

"You can. You have to." He put a bandage on her foot and rose. "There isn't anything beyond this cabin for us, Ashley. We've talked about this. I have to go after Valeri."

"But why?"

He stood there, fists clenched at his sides, as if battling an army of inner demons. "Because he might be able to tell me what happened to my cousin."

"Your—cousin? I thought you said you didn't have family."

"And I thought you were going to remember I'm a liar." He held up his hands as if to avoid an argument. "None of this matters, Ashley. The less you know, the better."

"I want to know." She wanted to know everything there was about Sawyer Paxton. She held out her hands, drew him into the chair across from her. "Tell me about your cousin. Start with a name."

"Georgiana. She is, was, nineteen. The daughter of my father's younger sister. She went to New York to check out colleges." He angled his chin down. "She wants to be a doctor. She and a friend went to a nightclub. Her friend came home. Georgiana didn't."

"I'm so sorry." She searched his face for what he must be feeling, but, much like he'd been when she'd first met him, he'd closed himself off. Even from her. "You think Valeri knows what happened to her?"

"The club she went to is owned by his brother. Marko's been convicted of human trafficking. I'd say chances are pretty good if he doesn't, he can find out."

"Oh, Sawyer." She swallowed around the sorrow. His family had to be in agony.

"I promised her mother. They're the only family I have left. And I never break my promises, Ashley. Never. No matter how much I might want to stay with you, stay hidden with you, I can't. Not when there's the slightest chance I can find Georgiana."

Ashley reached over, touched his face. "Of course. You have to do everything you can to find her. But isn't there another way? Couldn't you talk to the police or the FBI or someone who could help—"

"No matter how many times I ask, you just won't get your head out of the clouds, will you?" His smile, when it finally emerged, broke her heart. "The world works differently for us, Ashley. I live in the dark places you can't begin to imagine exist."

"Don't patronize me, Sawyer." That he thought her so pristine as to not understand how the real world worked had her pulling away. "I was married to a cop. My brother's a detective. And I've seen the worst people can do to one another most days I go to work. Don't tell me I don't know about dark places."

"You've spent the last few days trying to convince yourself I'm something other than what I am. And what I am is bad for you in every possible way." He got up and went to the fireplace and relit the fire he'd doused just yesterday.

"I refuse to believe that. What are you doing?"

"I'm making sure Taras and Javi find us sooner than later. I promised to get you home. This is how we're doing it."

"No. No, Sawyer, they'll kill you. They'll kill both of us."

He went to her, held her face in his hands and bored his gaze into hers. "They will not hurt you. Ever." He pressed his lips to her mouth.

She believed him. Again, she believed him without understanding why. "And what about you?"

"You have to trust me. I have an idea. A route out." He released her, reached for the poker and stoked the fire. Imagined or not, she heard the flames and smoke erupt up the chimney as if a signal flare had been fired.

"So now what do we do?" she demanded as a new wave of fear washed over her body and soul.

"Now we wait."

He stood, silent as a sentry, rifle in hand, looking into the darkness.

Slade had never realized how deafening the quiet could be. Never realized how much he appreciated the absence of anything other than the pulsing night and the creatures that inhabited it.

His stomach growled. Dinner had consisted of a combination of fire-warmed beans and anonymous meal packets which, if he had to lay odds, had been a kind of chicken concoction. He never thought he'd get to the point he missed prison food.

He'd hoped Taras and Javi would find them sooner rather than later. He wanted this over. He wanted to leave Ashley, and all the hope just the sight of her promised, behind. He wanted to forget that for a moment, he'd let himself believe this case would end with a happily-every-after.

Someone had betrayed him. Someone he'd trusted. Baxter? Flynn? Robeson? Someone higher up the chain of command? He couldn't be certain. Not even now that his identity was known to those who hunted him. The only person who could tell him the name of the person responsible was the one man who wanted him dead. This went beyond protecting Ashley at this point. Went beyond finding Georgiana. This was about protecting the agency he'd sworn his life to. If he'd been betrayed, what other information had been imparted?

How many other agents were in trouble?

Who, Slade wondered for what had to be the hundredth time, could he trust?

He heard rustling in the other room, glanced over his shoulder through the flickering candlelight that barely illuminated the cabin. There was only one person he could trust now. Ashley. And yet, he couldn't tell her the truth. If he died as Sawyer Paxton, out here in the middle of nowhere, he'd take his secret with him. If he lived, if he somehow survived the next few days, then he could tell her.

And maybe, if his luck held out, she'd forgive him.

Ashley emerged from the bedroom, the quilt from the bed wrapped around her like a shawl. The candlelight illuminated her from her glorious long blond hair to the tips of her toes, with their chipped red nail polish. She stood, leaning against the wall, watching him.

"They aren't coming tonight." Her voice was whisper soft.

"We don't know that." He turned his back on

her, unable to withstand seeing her in glowing per-
fection.

"I know it. Sawyer." She'd walked up behind
him and he hadn't heard. Didn't feel. Not until she
placed a hand on his arm. "Sawyer, come to bed."

He shook his head. The danger lurked, stalked.
Hunted. If he looked away, even for a moment,
they'd move in and take all that he cherished.

"You can either come to bed or listen to me bug
you for the rest of the night."

"You should be asleep."

"I can't sleep. Not anymore." She pushed herself
under his free arm, wrapped her own around his
waist and, after a gentle check of his bandage—a
move that brought a smile to his lips even now—
locked herself against him. "Not without you."

He squeezed his eyes shut. Words he didn't
want to hear. Words he couldn't accept. Words that
slipped in and around his heart and branded him.
He was, for as long as he lived, hers.

"Please, Sawyer." She spoke into the stillness.
"One more night. For me." She reached around him,
led him into the bedroom.

She pushed the quilt off her shoulders and stood
before him, naked, beautiful and welcoming. Her
hair spilled around her shoulders, catching the rays
of the moon shining through the window. Ashley
reached for him, drawing him in, putting her arms
around his neck and pulling his mouth down to

hers as she pressed every beautiful inch of herself against him.

There was no hiding his desire for her. No trying to stop his body from reacting as he bent and lifted her to him. Her lips teased his, tempted his, until he gave up resisting and opened for her, letting her take what she needed, what she wanted from him.

Between the tender, soul-deep kisses and the small steps toward the bed, his clothes landed on the floor beside the quilt. A solitary candle flickered against the motion between them, casting shadows on the aged wallpapered walls. He let her bring him onto the bed beside her, lay with her and tangled their legs together. She drew feather-light fingers down the side of his face, his neck, his shoulders. She traced every inch of him, dancing along his hip, his thigh, then detouring as a wicked smile played across her lips.

He mirrored her actions, memorizing every curve, every wondrous part of her body. The kiss that followed was one of melancholy. Of need. Of promise. Her tongue played with his, drawing him closer, deeper into her as she rolled onto her back, settling him over her.

Reason prickled from somewhere in the back of his thoughts. Practical reason he'd have preferred to silence, but he shifted away, reaching for a foil packet next to the candle, only to discover there weren't any more.

"It's okay." She slid her hand down his arm,

wound her fingers through his and drew his hand back to her body. "Just this time."

"Ashley—"

She kissed him. Silenced him. Convinced him.

"I've been tested but you can't be sure." He pulled back enough to look down at her, smoothed his hands through her hair, pressed gentle kisses along either side of her face. "I can't be—"

"I know what I want." She kept her gaze locked on his as he slipped, ever so gently, into her. She groaned, arched her neck and offered it to his waiting mouth. "This. I want this."

The tenderness, the bravery, the passion from her erased the last of his doubt and he gave in. With long, slow thrusts, he pressed himself into her, whispered her name and what he felt. The more he told her, the harder she breathed. Her pulse beat heavily against his lips as she locked her legs around his hips, her arms around his shoulders. She encompassed him. Cocooned him.

She'd saved him.

He found her mouth again, mimicking the motion of their bodies with his tongue.

Ashley drew him in so deep he didn't want to leave, couldn't bear the thought as she climbed, climbed, and broke free beneath him, the force of which had him climbing with her.

Until he lost himself in the storm.

Chapter 12

Ashley had withstood the calm before many storms, but none had ever felt quite so personal or foreboding as this one. She'd bid her share of good-byes over the years, yet none had felt this final and heart-wrenching.

She'd slept in Sawyer's arms, wrapped around him, holding him so close she couldn't tell where she ended and he began.

She loved him. It was that thought, or rather the utter acceptance of that thought, that brought her awake. The pale light shimmered through the window that overlooked the forest protecting and surrounding the cabin—the cabin that would forever be etched in her memory. If only she could freeze this moment, this peaceful moment, to make it last a lifetime.

Sawyer's hand trailed up and down her arm as his heartbeat pounded under her ear. Ashley squeezed her eyes shut, wanting to hold still for just one more…

"It's nearly noon. We should get up."

"I know," she whispered, but she lifted her hand, rested it under her cheek and felt his pulse against her palm. "It's today, isn't it."

He pressed his lips to the top of her head. "Valeri's meeting with his contact tonight. It's my last chance."

It was on the tip of her tongue to beg him to stay hidden away from the world, but she didn't. She couldn't. Not only because of the selfishness of the plea, but because he was right. She had a life she had to get back to. A life she had the chance to continue to live because of him.

"What happens after?" *If you survive.*

"Let's not think about that." He sat up, leaving her lying on the bed as he got to his feet.

"It's kind of hard not to think about that. Wait." She kicked out of the sheets and reached for him.

He caught her hands. "Ashley—"

"I'm checking your stitches, not getting frisky."

He chuckled and shook his head, lifting his arm so she could pry up the bandage and check the wound. "Looks okay. Should be fine in the shower." She knew the game they were playing; the odd tension in the room could only be broken by their addressing the truth of their situation, which neither of them seemed prepared to do. "I could supervise."

Another shake of his head. "I'll be quick."

He was. Soon, he emerged from the bathroom, showered and dressed, and looking as if he'd just stepped out from between the covers of a steamy romance novel. If there weren't two revenge-minded killers on their way, Ashley would have given serious consideration to unmaking the bed.

She gathered up her jeans, a clean T-shirt and her underwear, headed into the bathroom, and showered. As she climbed out of the tub, she heard an odd sound from the hallway. Fear surged through her system. She got dressed in a hurry, and slowly opened the door, ready for just about anything.

What she found, however, didn't quite register. The hallway was obscured by what looked like the back of a bookcase. She entered the narrow space that had been opened in the wall. "Sawyer?"

He jerked upright, swinging around, his hands filled with boxes of ammunition. "I thought you were in the shower."

"Doesn't take as long when it's just me." She was unable to see much beyond the glow of the flashlight that he'd perched on the edge of a desk. "What is this? A hidden room?"

"I'm guessing the previous occupant wasn't a fan of company."

He'd put the duffel bag in here, on the bed, with

the last of the medical supplies, bottled water and protein bars. She tried to ignore the dread that she suddenly sensed. "Is this where you found the guns?"

"Yes." He seemed to hesitate, then carried the boxes out.

"Why didn't you tell me about this?" She followed him, well aware of the answer although he refused to give it. "If you think I'm going to hide out in there like some incapable coward, think again."

"Taras is a killer, Ashley."

"Don't patronize me," she snapped. "I'm well aware. Why else did you give me shooting lessons if you weren't expecting me to help?"

He flinched, glanced away. "I told you. I wanted to make sure you could defend yourself."

"Try again." She moved in, hands planted on her hips, and glared up at him. "Sleeping with you hasn't suddenly changed who I am. Nor has it given you any input as to what I do with my life."

His lips twitched. "I didn't think it did."

"Don't you dare laugh." She poked at him, drove him back a couple of steps. "We are in this together until we aren't. Do you hear me?"

"You're a doctor, Ashley. You took an oath to do no harm. I will not put you in that position of having you be responsible for someone's death."

"I'm already responsible for one death," she reminded him even as the guilt and nausea swam in her empty stomach. The image of Bradley and the shock on his face when Valeri pulled the trigger made her sick.

"I have enough on my conscience already, Ashley. I'm not going to add anything else. When the time comes, you'll stay in that room until we're gone. You'll wait a good hour and then you're going to run and run and not stop until you flag down the first car you see. Call for help, call your brother to let him know you're safe. End of story." He grabbed the pistol he'd brought with him from the other cabin and dropped the magazine free, reloaded it.

"And if I refuse?"

He looked at her, and for a moment, the man she'd fallen in love with vanished behind a mask of disappointment and sadness. "You have to do it. It's the smart play. And you're no fool, Dr. Ashley McTavish." He cocked his weapon and set it beside the others.

"Sawyer—"

"I will not watch you die." His whisper was more plea than demand. Her heart constricted, as if it had forgotten how to beat.

"Sawyer—" She stepped toward him, but he backed away.

"Please, Ashley. I am begging you. I couldn't stand it if you were hurt or worse. There is nothing, nothing that would cause me more pain and Taras will know that the instant he sees us together." Now he did come to her, and cupped her cheek in his hand, stroked his thumb against the corner of her mouth. "If I know you're okay, if I know you're safe, I can do what I need to. That's how you can help." He held out the pistol she'd used for target practice yesterday. "Keep this with you at all times. Don't let it out of your sight. And when I tell you to go, you go and you pull that door closed behind you. If anyone other than me comes through that door, you know what to do."

Angry, frustrated tears blurred her vision. She blinked them back, reveling in the feel of his hand against her skin. And the love she saw shining in his eyes. "I don't want to lose you," she said softly. "Tell me there's a way—"

"There isn't." His expression became hard before he turned his back to her. "There never was. The sooner you accept that, the better off you'll be."

From somewhere close to the house came the sound of snapped branches.

"No," Ashley murmured. *Not now. Not so soon.* "Sawyer?"

He grabbed the shotgun and pumped the slide. "Go." He didn't look back.

An eerie calm descended. A calm that didn't quite settle until Slade watched Ashley pull the secret door closed behind her. He hated the look of rejection he'd seen on her face. He wasn't rejecting her, though. It was every protective instinct he had surging to the surface. He knew the odds for Georgiana. Chances were she was dead or lost to her family forever, but Ashley was neither. And as long as he had breath in his body, he was going to keep her from harm.

Slade shoved the pistol in the back of his waist-band, picked up the shotgun and headed to the front door. He strained to hear the footsteps rus-tling against the dried leaves he'd piled up in front of the cabin.

He took long, slow breaths, letting go of all the regrets, all the disappointments. He'd made mis-takes. He hadn't been perfect. But he'd done the best he could. That would have to do.

The next crunch of leaves had him reaching for the handle on the door. He clicked the lever, swung open the door. The morning breeze flooded in, chilling him to the bone.

He moved into the center of the open doorway. And then, as Taras and Javi both kept their guns aimed at his chest, he set his shotgun down. And held up his hands.

"Kill me and Valeri will never find out how much information got passed along." He kept his voice low, knowing that the hidden room was well insulated, but didn't want to take a chance. "He must be curious about how much we know."

"He's right," Javi said, moving a step closer, his dark eyes unwavering. "Valeri will want to ques-tion him."

"Valeri wants him dead," Taras said. "And the sooner the better."

"I've been with Valeri for more than a year," Slade interjected. "And I've paid attention. Take me to him. If he wants to get rid of me, he can do it himself."

Taras inclined his head as if considering the idea. "Where's the doctor?"

Slade's heart pounded so hard he felt certain they would hear it. Especially Javi, as he crept closer to the door. "Gone. I sent her away yesterday. By now the police have her."

"Unlikely. If they did, we'd have heard about it on the news." Taras motioned to Javi. "Check the cabin. If he's lying, they both pay the price right here."

Slade stepped aside to allow Javi to pass. He noticed Javi still held his injured arm close to his chest. It took all of Slade's control to keep from watching every step the guy took. Instead, Slade pinned his attention on Taras, who looked as if he'd gone a few rounds with a bear. "Rough couple of days?"

"I've had better." Taras's eyes were almost bloodshot. "I've had worse."

Slade could hear Javi kicking chairs, shifting the table, knocking against the walls. He turned slightly and froze, watching. Javi ducked into the bedroom, then the bathroom. He emerged, saying nothing, but stopped and looked at Slade, who didn't blink and barely breathed.

Javi tried the closet next, and when he didn't

immediately move on to somewhere else, Slade's instincts roared. Javi smoothed his fingers against the scars in the wall.

"What's taking so long? She in there or not?" Taras yelled.

Slade evaluated his options. The shotgun was close enough but he'd only get off one round before Taras or Javi took him down. The semiautomatic pistol at his back would result in the same outcome. Taras or Javi? He knew whose shot was better; he wasn't sure which of the two should live. But could he do it in time?

"Just checking something," Javi yelled back, his gaze meeting Slade's. He moved slowly and shoved his gun into his jeans.

Slade could then hear Javi using his fingers to trace along the sides of the closet. It was only a matter of time before Javi found the edge.

Javi's fingers paused.

Slade stopped breathing. He recognized the following sound.

Javi had pulled the hidden door open.

"What is it? What did you find?" Taras hollered as Slade remained frozen. His fingers twitched. "Javi?"

Javi must have disappeared inside.

Ashley stood pressed against the far wall, directly across from the door, slightly ajar now, pistol gripped in her hands. The dimness and close air threatened to suffocate her. The seconds ticked by.

If anyone other than me comes through that door, you know what to do. Sawyer's words echoed in her mind. Her hands shook. His warning, his caution to her, had been on point. The idea, even if shooting in self-defense, had her questioning everything she knew about herself.

The door scraped more fully open.

Ashley swallowed a gasp and held her arms straight out as a stream of light moved across the floor.

If anyone other than me comes through that door, you know what to do.

A shadow moved into view. A shadow wider and shorter than Sawyer. Fear coated her in a cold sweat. The metal was even cool against her skin. Her eyes adjusted to the light and the face came into focus. Javi.

They looked each other straight in the eye. She could see her hands shaking, but she wouldn't give in. She wouldn't let them hurt her and not in front of Sawyer. It was all he'd asked of her.

"Javi?" Taras's voice sounded faint but demanding. "What's going on? Is she in there? I said, what did you find?"

"A secret room," Javi shouted in response. "Must have been where he found the guns."

"What about the doctor?" Taras asked with straining patience.

"Javi, please," Ashley whispered. "You know what he'll do."

Javi stared at her for what seemed like hours. Finally, Javi stepped out of the room. As he did, he motioned for her to move out of the light. She scrambled to the side, hopped onto the bottom bunk and curled her legs in beneath her. Javi threw something at her, something she barely caught before it rattled to the floor.

Her hands shook as she realized what it was. A phone. Tears of relief blurred her eyes as words of gratitude froze in her throat.

Javi closed the door, but not all the way. "She's not here. Lucky's telling us the truth."

Ashley still couldn't breathe.

"We might find her on our way. Doesn't seem right to call you Lucky anymore, given your luck's run out," Taras goaded. "And it's the last thing you'll be when Valeri's done with you. Let's go. We've got a long ride ahead of us. Javi, you coming?"

"Right behind you." Footfalls echoed out of the cabin.

"Keep him safe," she said, sending the wish out into the universe. "Please keep him safe." Her breath returned in shudders so sharp her ribs ached. Only when she was certain she was alone did she start to count.

"Don't touch that." Vince Sutton, arms crossed over his chest, feet resting on the console of the computer terminal in the surveillance van, didn't even open his eyes when Jack reached over to adjust the focus on one of the cameras. "You want to play with toys, Chloe Ann has a whole roomful."

Eamon grinned at Jack's grumbling response. The surveillance van wasn't quite as snazzy as the FBI ones he was used to, but Vince had done a decent job with this one at the last minute so they could observe the port. SAC Don Harrison had approved Vince's, Cole's and Jack's participation in the stakeout, if for no other reason than he believed Eamon's claim that if they didn't keep tabs on Jack, he'd probably go down to the pier and rip the place apart searching for his sister.

As it was, they were one of four surveillance teams in the area. A command center had been set up a few blocks away in an old construction trailer so as not to bring attention to the mission. The command center was where Don and his agents were holed up.

Don was also able to get an additional truck disguised and stationed as a food truck inside the port, which also gave them ears on the dockworkers.

The rotating, blinking screens lit up the back of the van like strobe lights. Monitoring those screens had given Eamon a headache that pounded behind his eyes.

Though it wasn't as big a headache as confirming that Agent Caleb Flynn was most definitely on the Valeri payroll. Once his fellow agents—trusted agents from Don's group—had known where to look, thanks to Vince, a whole lot was revealed and was going to land Flynn, if not in the witness-protection program, certainly in prison.

Three grown men in the back of an increasingly close van, however, was starting to try everyone's patience. After only a day together, Eamon, Jack and Vince—or the van—weren't smelling particularly fresh. They'd blown through the snack food and sodas in record time, with a bag full of garbage awaiting disposal by the back door.

"I should have gone with Cole," Jack muttered and purposely flicked a dormant switch on the board.

"Not going to argue with you." Vince leaned his head back and closed his eyes. "No word on the search?"

Eamon checked his phone. "Sarah said she'd call if they had anything new to report." Sending Sarah out to coordinate with the agents continuing to search for Valeri and the rest of the escapees had seemed the best course of action. Every angle of the case needed attention. He was determined that nothing would be left undone or untried.

"You're convinced Baxter's been in the dark about Flynn?" Jack asked.

"There's no evidence he has any idea." What Baxter did have, however, was a serious case of resentment because the investigation had been taken over by Harrison. Harrison had in turn relegated

Baxter, Robeson and Flynn to sticking to their offices downtown. "That said, the blowback's gonna sting big-time. If he knew, he's complicit. If he didn't…" Eamon let that thought trail off.

"Any chance you can have Jason pick up a take-out order and make a delivery?" Jack asked Vince in an overly sweet tone. "I'm starving."

Vince smirked. "After dark."

Eamon peered out one of the windows in the back. "Still got a couple of hours to go before then. I think there's beef jerky—"

Jack's cell phone buzzed. He looked down at the screen. "Unknown number."

"Answer it," Eamon ordered.

Jack glared at him as if he didn't need to be told. "I'll even put it on speaker, so we can all hear, okay?" He tapped the screen. "McTavish."

"It's me, Jack. It's Ash."

"Ashley?" Jack jumped to his feet and smashed his head against the roof of the van. "Ow!" He dropped the phone, clutched his head and stepped back, knocking over his seat. Vince dived to retrieve the phone and held it out to them. "Ashley, where are you?" Jack stomped around the van nursing his head. "Are you safe? Are you hurt?"

"I'm okay. I'm fine. I'm—" she sobbed. "Sorry. It's just so good to hear your voice. It feels like years."

Jack nodded, as if he couldn't find the strength or the words to speak.

"Ashley, it's Agent Eamon Quinn with the FBI. Do you remember me?" Eamon motioned for Vince to help Jack, who had missed his chair and hit the floor with a thud.

"Yes, of course."

"Do you know where you are?" Eamon asked.

"Not exactly. Lassen National Forest is what Sawyer said. There's a map here in the cabin—"

"Cabin. You're in a cabin?" Eamon logged on to one of the laptops and brought up a map of the forest.

"Yes. We were in a different one before. With Valeri and the others. Then Sawyer and I got away, swam across a big lake. There's another lake where I am now. I think we went east of the first lake. Toward the sunrise."

"All right." Eamon compared the data they had from where they'd already searched.

"Hold up. Go back. Here." Vince tapped on the screen, then grabbed one of the file folders. "That's only about five miles from where her watch went dead."

"You were able to track my watch. Jack?" Ashley called. "Are you there?"

"Yeah, here." Jack groaned. "Gave myself a concussion."

"No way can we ping her cell phone in that dense area," Vince said.

"Let me go outside," Ashley offered.

"Ashley, what's the number on the phone you're

using?" Vince asked when she confirmed she was outside.

"Hang on." After a few seconds, she rattled it off for him. "Does that help?"

Vince nodded, tapping in the number on a search engine. "I've got three, no, four cell phones in that area. Faint. But they're there. I'm going to send the information to Cole in the chopper."

"Getting it to Sarah, too. Ashley," Eamon said, "we've got help coming your way, okay? Might take them some time. I want you to go somewhere safe."

"I am safe. Sawyer, he made sure they took him without me. He saved my life."

Eamon glanced at Vince, then Jack. Neither seemed to know what to say any more than he did. "All right, Ashley. We can talk about that once we get you back. We're going to have Cole get you whatever you need and bring you to the hospital, okay?"

"No."

"No?" Jack blasted. "What do you mean no?"

Eamon reached over and quieted his friend.

"There's a meeting between Valeri and someone in his organization," Ashley told them. "That's where Sawyer's going. That's where he wanted to go."

"What does that have to do with you?" Jack asked.

"I want to be there. I need to be there. With Sawyer. I mean, after. Please. Before you take him away again, I need to see him."

"Ashley—"

"I know what I'm asking, Jack. I understand.

Please. I won't get in the way. Just…don't let anything happen to him."

"We'll do what we can to protect him, Ashley," Eamon jumped in. "I promise. And meanwhile, we'll let Cole know what's happening."

"Jack?" Ashley seemed to want her brother's confirmation.

"Yeah. All right, Ashley." Jack shook his head. "Keep the line open, okay? We don't want to lose the signal on the GPS."

"Okay."

Eamon muted Jack's phone. "She doesn't know about Slade."

"He didn't tell her." Vince cringed. "There must be a reason."

"I'm not going to question it." Eamon's mind raced. "I need to bring Harrison up to speed." He pulled out his own phone. "Vince, let me know when Cole's found Ashley."

Chapter 13

With the weapon still in her hand, Ashley sat at the cabin's kitchen table, barely registering the *whap-whap-whap* of helicopter blades overhead. She knew, from a medical standpoint, that she was in shock. Ridiculous, she kept telling herself even as she heard the rumble of engines and slamming doors. She was fine. She was alive.

But Bradley wasn't. And Sawyer... She blinked and sent a tear trickling down her cheek. The idea of never seeing him again...

"Ashley?"

She hadn't heard him come in. Ashley looked up and found Detective Cole Delaney standing in front of her, the mixed expression of relief and uncertainty marring his features. "Hey." Cole motioned with his hand. The men and women behind him stopped, remained where they were. He crouched in front of her. "Hey, Ashley? Can I have that?"

"Huh?" She blinked again, wishing the fog around her brain would dissipate. "Oh. Yeah, sure." She looked down at the gun, where he'd laid his hand over hers. "Sorry. I'd like it back." Funny. It seemed to be the only thing she had to connect her with Sawyer.

"Okay. We'll see about that." He pried her fingers free and handed the weapon over his shoulder to a tech, who bagged it. "I've got a helicopter waiting about a mile from here to take you to the hospital."

"No." She shook her head, finally coming out of the daze. "No, I spoke to Jack, and Eamon, and I need to be there. I need to see Sawyer again."

"They told me." He stood and gently pulled her to her feet. "We know you do, but first things first. We need to make sure you're okay. Do this for us, all right? Do it for Jack. He's been a mess worrying about you."

"I'm sorry." The tears welled, and no matter how hard she tried, she couldn't stop them. "I didn't mean... I didn't think. The bus. I just stopped to help. I needed to help." One choice, just one blink-of-an-eye choice, and her entire life had changed.

"We know, Ash." Cole pulled her against him and held her close. "It's all right. You did good."

"Valeri killed Bradley. The guard." She held on

to Cole, her fingers gripping his shirt as she began to shake. "Right in front of me. I couldn't stop him."

Cole said something over her head, his voice low, before he turned the two of them toward the door. "We're going to get you taken care of, Ashley. Greta and Allie are going to meet us at the hospital. You can talk to them if you need to. About anything that might have happened."

"Might have—" Her confusion didn't last long. She recognized that look on Cole's face. "Sawyer didn't hurt me. Cole, don't let anyone think—"

"All right." He ran his hand down her arm. "What about the others? Did they hurt you?"

"No. Sawyer protected me. I guess I protected myself, too, in a way." Sawyer. What was happening to him? Where was he? Where had Taras and Javi taken him? "You have to find Sawyer, Cole. You can't let them kill him. They're going to. They know something about him. Something bad."

He led her to one of the waiting SUVs.

"What exactly did they say, Ashley? About Sawyer?" Cole asked, holding the door open for her.

"Um." She pressed her fingers to her temple, tried to think. "The other night when they took us outside, Sawyer said something like 'You know, don't you,' and Valeri said he did. He'd known, but not long enough. What does that even mean?" It should make sense. But nothing made sense right now.

"We'll explain everything after you've been checked out. I'll just be a minute, okay?" He closed the door, but she watched as he spoke to the agents and the forensics team flooding the small cabin.

The cabin that, for a while, had been paradise. And would now only be a memory.

On the floor of a panel van was not, Slade concluded, the ideal way to travel. He tried to sit upright. His hands had gone numb thanks to the cable tie locking them behind his back.

Taras drove fast, but not likely fast enough to risk being pulled over by police. Given the public's thirst for reality crime stories, Slade would bet interest in the escaped convicts had only increased, which could work to Slade's advantage. Although, despite his desire to be free of the two of them, Slade hoped the roadblocks and checkpoints were no more. He still had a shot with Valeri and was determined to see this through to the end no matter what. Taras turned onto the highway and soon they were zooming back into the valley, the afternoon sun blasting heat through the tinted windows.

Since being tossed into the back of the van, he'd had plenty of time to do what he did best: think. Reflect. Evaluate. And there was a lot that didn't add up. Not where one person was concerned. The fact that Javi had lied to Taras about Ashley's hiding sparked his curiosity. He should have had Javi on his radar more these past few months. Maybe it could now be his chance to get out of this alive?

If there was one thing Slade understood with

complete comprehension, it was how difficult balancing the two sides of your soul could be when working deep undercover.

"How about a little real music," Slade yelled up to Taras, who had country blasting out of the speakers. Slade had to bite back a grin of triumph when Taras turned up the volume. "Thank you!" He turned his attention to Javi, who sat across from him on a bench seat, pistol on his lap, his head tilted back and his eyes closed as if he was asleep. He wasn't.

Slade knocked his knee against Javi's. "Why?"

"Why what?" Javi's lips barely moved.

"You know why what. Ashley. Why'd you lie to Taras?" He was betting his life that question wouldn't land him any deeper in the swamp than he was currently drowning in.

Javi shrugged. "You know there's nothing Marko loathes more than a snitch. He's gonna kill you long and slow."

"That's Special Agent Snitch to you." It felt good to say the words again. The façade he'd been living shattered like an antique mirror and oddly enough, his chest loosened. He could breathe again. "As long as he or Olena doesn't come within ten feet of Ashley, they can do their worst to me."

"Odd thing for a Fed to say."

"Odd thing for a criminal to do. Protect an innocent." He tried to roll his shoulders, but the numbing pain only settled more firmly in his arms. "Did Baxter send you in?"

Javi rolled his head to the side and opened his eyes.

"Okay. Not FBI." Slade glanced up at Taras, who was preoccupied with crossing multiple lanes of traffic. "Local cop? DEA?" With the Valeris' suspected involvement in human trafficking, it wouldn't surprise him. "Customs?"

Javi snorted and returned to feigning sleep. "You run out of acronyms, Lucky? You forgot ATF."

"Should have started with that one. Sorry."

Javi's lips twitched. "The Valeri brothers have been moving into arms dealing. Only way we could get close was once Marko got sent up. Money from their trafficking operation's funding the arms transactions. Trading one evil for another. Maybe tonight we stop both."

One could only hope. "How'd you pin me as a cop?"

"That protective streak you've got runs pretty deep. Had a good idea when you saved me from that pummeling the night I went inside. A couple of well-directed questions by my handler confirmed it. You're good. Unless a beautiful doctor gets involved. You lost your edge once she showed up."

Lost his edge? More like found a reason to live. His life had been consumed with finding Georgiana for so long, he hadn't been able to see beyond it, whatever lay beyond the answers he needed to find.

And then Dr. Ashley McTavish turns up, bright as a beacon as if lighting his way. "You aren't just telling me this to get me to lower my guard and confess all my sins against Marko, are you?"

Javi spared a glance at Taras, who had apparently given up caring whether he hit light speed on the freeway. "Your cousin's alive."

Javi couldn't have surprised him more if he'd tried. "How do you know? *What* do you know? Where is she?"

"Chill," Javi snapped. "I'll clarify. She was alive as of three months ago. She managed to get a message out when she was in Caracas. Authorities got there too late, but the info got passed to the manager, who…so on and so on."

"What did the message say?" Slade's stomach twisted itself into knots. He didn't want to know. He needed to know.

"Just your name, FBI and that she was alive. We tried to reach out, but were told you were on indefinite leave. Interpol's on it. They'll find her. And hopefully others."

A weight that had landed on his chest two years earlier suddenly lifted.

"That enough to keep you breathing?" Javi asked.

"I already had a reason." Slade didn't miss the quick grin on his fellow law enforcement agent's face.

The music lowered and Taras looked over his

shoulder, eyes glinting like daggers. "What are you two talking about?"

"Just finding out what he knows," Javi said with a shrug. "He's not talking."

"He will." Taras's teeth flashed. "Once Olena gets a hold of him, he'll tell us everything."

Ashley finally understood why people hated hospitals. At least, she did from the frustrated patient's perspective. She'd been examined from head to toe, had blood drawn, the works. The semiprivate room was all private thanks to the absence of a roommate. The doctor and nurse had both urged her to get some sleep, but that wasn't going to happen. Not until she knew what was happening with Sawyer.

She dumped her clothes out of the big plastic bag, stripped, and put on her jeans and T-shirt, stuffed her feet into the sneakers. What had happened to her bags? Her car? Was everything evidence now? Part of her wanted to scream at the universe to turn back the clock, to stop herself from hopping out of her car to help whoever was on that bus. But the rest of her, the part of her that couldn't push even the thinnest thought of Sawyer out of her mind, clung to the past few days like a life preserver in a hurricane.

"Ashley?" The soft rap on the doorframe had her looking up from lacing her shoes. The dark-haired woman stood just outside, kind, familiar eyes assessing even as she silently asked for entry. With her hands clasped behind her back, the soft butter yellow of her skirt-and-sweater set felt oddly comforting among the whites and grays of the hospital room. "How are you doing?"

"Is that Dr. Allie Hollister-Kellan asking?" Ashley inquired with a bit of bite. "Or the Allie who usually shows up at my place with my favorite bottle of wine? Boy, that's a mouthful of a name. Why did you hyphenate, anyway?"

"Actually," Allie said, "Max suggested it. He hyphenated his, too. Says it's the only way he'll ever be called doctor of anything. Are you going somewhere?"

Ashley rested an arm on her knee. "Jack said I could observe whatever's going on where Valeri's concerned. So, you tell me. Where am I going?"

"How about we talk first?" Allie leaned against the doorframe, that calm, irritatingly understanding expression locked in place.

"Nothing to talk about. I'm fine."

"All right. Then how about you let Greta talk?"

"Greta? She's here?"

"I couldn't keep her away." Allie looked over her shoulder, and in the next second, Ashley's sister-in-law breezed into the room. Greta Renault, who had neither hyphenated nor taken her husband's name, hadn't waited to be invited in. Instead, she swooped toward Ashley and enveloped her in a hug so tight, Ashley blinked back tears. Sawyer had been right. She was loved.

"I was so scared," Greta whispered when Ashley returned the hug. "When Jack called to say you were okay…" She stepped back, put some distance between them and swiped at her cheeks. "I'm sorry. I told myself I wouldn't do this. I'm just glad you're all right. We all are."

Ashley took hold of Greta's hand and squeezed. "Me, too." She glanced at Allie. "The doctor suggested I talk to a psychiatrist. Is that why you're here?" Did her brother and the doctor assume she'd be more amenable to someone she knew?

"I'm here because you're my friend, Ashley. And I'll be here in whatever capacity you need me to be. That said…" Allie came forward and closed the door, then set a brown paper bag on the table at the foot of the bed. "It's a family tradition when one of us is stuck in the hospital. Bagels from Schofields. Cinnamon raisin. I applied a bit of pressure and got them to bake fresh."

Ashley eyed the bag. Even though she hadn't eaten all day, she wasn't hungry. But as a doctor— and as a friend—she retrieved the offering and sat back down by the window.

"Eden and Simone are at the station helping gather more information on…well, on a lot of aspects of the case." Allie sat on the edge of the bed, prim and proper, and looking only a tad uncomfortable. "They send their best. Eden didn't think you'd be up to being swarmed with affection right off the bat. They sent Greta as their surrogate."

"I live to please," Greta said, a teasing lilt in her

voice. "Oh, wow. This is a great view of the city."
She clicked open the blinds and cupped her hands
around her face so she could look out. "Interesting
dichotomy between the hospital and the world outside. All those twinkling lights and night sky make
it seem almost surreal."

"I sense a new series of paintings in the offing."
Ashley's laugh sounded shaky even to her own ears.
Every experience Greta had seemed to add to her
cache of original artwork, which was in high demand
around the world. Rather than address Allie's assessing gaze, Ashley focused on the bagel, which was
still warm enough to make her mouth water. "Thanks
for these." She held out the bag. "You want one?"

"Ah, no." Allie cringed and seemed to turn a
bit green. "Raisins and I don't get along. Cole said
you seemed a little shaky back at the cabin where
they found you."

"Adrenaline crash. Delayed stress reaction."
Ashley shrugged. She was well aware how the body
reacted to circumstances like the ones she'd been
in. "All those agents swarming around me at the
cabin made it hard to breathe."

"I'll bet it did. All the more reason for you to stay
here overnight. Just as a precaution."

"I don't want to stay overnight." And she was a
little surprised Allie suggested it. "I want to know
what's happening with Sawyer."

Allie shook her head. "I don't have any information on that."

"Then I'll call Jack and ask him directly. Let me borrow your cell."

"Tell me about him. About Sawyer," Allie urged.

Ashley didn't want to share anything about any of her time with Sawyer. Her memories were, quite possibly, the only thing she would have left of him after tonight. "I know what he's done, if that's what you're asking. I also know what he did for me." The urge to defend him came as naturally to her as breathing. She tore off a chunk of bagel. "I wouldn't be alive if it wasn't for him."

"For that, we should all be grateful. I've read Marko Valeri's file."

The bagel turned to dust in her mouth.

"Sawyer gave me the details. He wanted me prepared. He wanted me to be aware of exactly who I was dealing with." And she really didn't want to relive all that now. "What's with all the questions, Allie? Is this some kind of stalling tactic to stop me from seeing Sawyer again?"

"You love him." Greta turned from the window, aimed sympathetic, understanding eyes on her. "You love him, don't you, Ashley?"

"I—" Trapped, she set the bag down. "Yes." It felt futile to turn away from the truth. The light that should have glowed inside of her refused to shine. Everything was so…complicated. "I love him. I don't understand it. I don't know how it happened, but it did…" She trailed off, hating the tears that fell from her eyes. She pressed a fist against her chest. "And it hurts. It's not supposed to hurt, is it?"

Greta moved closer, sat on the arm of the chair and rested her hands on Ashley's shoulders.

"You have to tell her, Allie," Greta murmured. "She has a right to know."

"A right to know what?" Abject terror seized Ashley from head to toe. She stood up so fast the bakery bag fell on the floor. "What is it? Is he hurt? Is he—" She stopped, steeled herself and pushed out the last of the thought. "Is he dead?"

"No, it's not that." Allie took a deep breath and folded her hands in her lap. "I know Jack and Eamon wanted to be the ones to tell you, but Greta's right. Given what you've shared with us, knowing how you feel about him, you need to know."

"If one of you doesn't tell me in the next few seconds—"

"The man you know as Sawyer Paxton doesn't exist, Ashley."

She felt the terror forming in her veins as Allie continued. "What are you talking about? He's real. I—"

"His real name is Slade Palmer, Ashley. He's an undercover agent with the FBI."

Chapter 14

Slade had to give Javi credit. The ATF undercover agent knew how to put on a show. Primarily, Slade thought, just as Javi yanked open the van door, at Slade's expense.

He hit the cement floor face-first; heard and felt his nose break. Blood poured down his cheek. His arms and hands had gone numb long before. To stop from suffocating, he shoved himself onto his back, choked on the blood trickling down his throat. Even as he wondered how he was going to stand, he was hauled up, dragged and thrown into a chair. The ties were cut, then new ones locked around his wrists and more tied him to the slatted chair.

Once his head stopped spinning, he forced his

eyes wide. The curved roofline, notched walls, cement floor and an echo-chamber feel that hurt his ears had him thinking airplane hangar. Given Valeri's penchant for solitude and the length of time Slade had been in the back of that van, Slade figured they were in or around what used to be McClellan Air Force Base, which had been closed for a number of years.

There was a makeshift kitchen, across the expanse of the hangar. Army-surplus cots and bedding nearby. Not a lot of baggage or collectibles. Clearly they were only here for the short term.

"Gotta say, Valeri." Slade spit blood onto the floor. "I prefer your last accommodations much better. This place doesn't have any character at all."

He expected the punch. Braced himself for it. Finding Olena on the other end of the fist that had cracked against his jaw, however? That was a surprise.

"FBI Special Agent Slade Palmer." Valeri stood slightly in front of Taras and Javi, arms crossed over his chest, looking as healthy as a Russian ox. Figured he'd have resiliency. Nothing was going to keep him down for long. "How very nice to make your acquaintance."

Slade spit again, looked up at Olena. "Is that the best you've got?"

She punched him again, this one sending pain rocketing against his eye. But it got him what he wanted. He felt the back of the chair give. Just a bit. But enough.

"Okay, Olena. We want him to be able to talk."

"Where's my little buddy Badger?" Slade turned his head.

"Attending to other matters," Valeri said. "What does the FBI know?"

"No idea." His head snapped back at the next punch. "You haven't exactly been a font of information. Careful." He could feel the bruises forming on his face. "You're going to ruin your manicure, Olena."

Olena gripped his face in one hand, her fingers digging into his skin. "Where is she?"

Slade searched for something beyond rage in Olena's dark eyes. What had happened to her that had turned her into this? "Somewhere you will never find her." He hoped she saw it. He hoped she understood. That he would gladly go to his grave to protect Ashley.

Olena grimaced. She yanked her hand away. Slade flexed his arms, felt the rungs on the back of the chair ease again.

"The Feds must have her," Taras said. "She's irrelevant now. We need to get moving. Edik will be waiting for us."

Edik.

Slade drew in a deep, cleansing breath. Finally. Despite veering severely off course, the plan to draw Edik out of hiding had finally transpired.

Marko's brother, the mastermind behind the entire operation, had left his hiding spot to come get his little brother out of trouble. Just as Baxter and the federal prosecutor had anticipated. Just as Slade had banked on to help him bring down the whole gang. He was close, so close. But Slade's odds of surviving the brotherly reunion were dropping with each second that passed. He'd accepted that possibility when he'd agreed to the undercover job.

But that had been before the bus crashed. Before…Ashley.

Ashley. Slade's heart warmed. Whatever happened, she'd been his salvation. His promise. His love.

The only regret he had was that she'd only know the truth about him after he was gone. He could only imagine the future they might have had together.

"We've got three hours to get to the port." Taras waved his gun in Slade's direction. "I say we end him here."

"This is getting repetitive," Slade managed to say despite his swollen mouth. "Make up your mind already."

"No." Valeri pushed Taras aside. "He may still be of some use to us. What better shield to have should we run into resistance than a federal agent. Besides, Edik will have other questions for him."

"If I get a say in this," Slade slurred, "I'd rather stay here."

This time it was Javi who sprang forward and drove his fist into Slade's gut. The breath surged out of his lungs. He didn't dare look at the other agent for fear of giving Javi away. He wanted to be there for the takedown, but if he couldn't, he firmly believed Javi would finish the job for him. The rungs on the chair cracked as he pulled his arms forward.

Slade planted his feet, pushed up and whipped the chair to the side. The chair exploded against Javi, shattering and freeing Slade. He dived forward, knocking Javi off his feet, tackling him to the ground. Javi kicked out and sent Slade flying. Slade slowed when something hot and metallic hit him in the left shoulder.

He smelled the blood this time. Looked down as he pitched forward and saw it at his feet.

"Get him in the car," Valeri ordered. "Javi, in the back. Keep him alive as long as you can. Olena, you drive."

Javi sliced through the restraints on Slade's wrists, put his arm over his shoulder and half dragged him to the van. "You are either very dumb or very brilliant. You should be dead."

Slade gasped when Javi dropped him into the seat Ashley had occupied days before. "Don't worry," he told the undercover agent. "I'm getting there."

It all made a strange, heartbreaking kind of sense. Ashley followed Allie and a uniformed officer, Deputy Scott Bowman, out of the elevator and into the major crimes department of the Sacramento Police Department. She didn't remember much about the ride over, or about anything that had been said after hearing that Sawy—no, *Slade*—was a highly decorated undercover FBI agent.

"You doing okay?" Allie draped an arm across Ashley's shoulders when they stopped by a closed conference room door. "I know you've had a lot to deal with in a very short amount of time. We're here for you. Whatever you need."

"Nothing has changed. I need to talk to him." Now more than ever. Why hadn't he told her? Why hadn't he trusted her? He'd let her fall in love with a criminal. How was she supposed to move past the idea he'd lied to her from the instant they'd met?

Allie nodded. "You have the right people trying to make that happen. Eamon's the best of the best. So's your brother and Cole."

The conference room door swung open. The compact middle-aged man who stood on the other side offered her an understanding smile. "Ashley. It's nice to see you again."

"Lieutenant Santos." She'd met Jack's boss on a few social occasions. "Is there any word? Does anyone know where Sawy—" darn it! "—Agent Palmer is?"

"We know where they're going to be, we just don't know when. In the meantime, we're hoping you can help us." He waved her inside, where she found Eden, Simone and a handful of other officers tapping away on computers and pinning up pictures and scribbling notes on giant dry-erase boards. "We're trying to put the pieces together. I know you're still waiting to give your official statement—"

"Allie said the FBI wants to take that."

"Agent Baxter will be here shortly to do just that."

"Ashley. We're so glad you're safe." Simone walked around the table and gave her a quick hug. "Have you had anything to eat?"

"Allie brought me a cinnamon-raisin bagel," Ashley said.

"From Schofields?" Eden held a file folder in one hand and rocked her daughter's car seat with the other. "They're the best. Especially when you're in the hospital."

"I'll have to take your word for it." Her stomach had rebelled almost instantly at the revelation about Slade. Something had to give when everything she'd believed in was exposed as a lie.

"Oh." Eden blinked. "Sorry about that. We can get you something now."

"I can do it." Allie rubbed her back.

"That'd be great."

Ashley claimed a chair by Eden and Chloe Ann, who was kicking her feet and chewing on a teething ring.

"I thought she might be a good dose of medicine

for you," Eden explained, nodding at her daughter. "You okay? Cole said you were no worse for wear."

Given who and what Valeri was, she should count herself lucky… A bubble of hysteria lodged in her chest. Lucky. Always appreciative of Eden's straightforward approach, Ashley managed a smile. "I'm fine." Nevertheless, she reached over and held out her finger for the baby. Chloe Ann gave a squeal and grabbed hold. "What do you all need help with?"

"We're trying to figure out how the cabin you were taken to connects back to Valeri." Eden released her hold on the carrier and tacked another document onto the board. "We're looking into anyone who's had contact with the escaped convicts. Hence the very awkward family tree here. So far the guards who were on Valeri's payroll were basically dead ends. They were offered big payouts once Valeri was out of the country. Wouldn't bet on that happening. Still, we figure it has to be someone who had contact with Valeri inside. We've run the warden, the staff, the medical personnel—"

Eden's voice faded as Ashley scanned the board of interconnected information. The photos looked like mug shots, but of course they were copies of driver's license photos. Easy to get the two confused. Names and dates were written below each. Some had check marks, others nothing of notation.

She stood, took her time examining the other

pictures and tidbits of info. Though not from the prison, but from the investigation into Marko Valeri.

"This is about the human-trafficking operation, isn't it?"

"Yes." Simone sat on the edge of the conference table. The DA always looked über-professional. "Eamon got us as much information as the FBI was willing to provide. It's more than we anticipated. But it's also like playing a master game of six degrees of separation."

Ashley lifted her fingers, brushed them across the face of the man she loved. His real face. Special Agent Slade Palmer bore little resemblance to Sawyer Paxton. The scar was new, obviously. As was the shaggy shoulder-length hair she'd plunged her hands into many times. The beard had concealed what she expected, handsome, breathtaking features that almost concealed the shadows in his eyes. *Where are you? Why didn't you tell me?*

"Baxter was in charge of the case," Lieutenant Santos said as she moved down the board. "That's his team. Agent Tony Robeson. Agent Caleb—"

Ashley stopped and stared. The eyes. Those familiar, fathomless eyes. "Do you know him?" Eden demanded. "We're pretty sure he's the agent who leaked Slade's real identity."

"I've never seen him before. But her?" She pointed to the board displaying the prison employees. She'd missed it at first, the face of the woman who would have easily stabbed her for…what? Ashley still didn't know. Her hair was bright red in the picture, long, wavy. Her nurse's uniform simple and nondescript. She took the agent's photo and tacked it onto the board next to the nurse's. "Here's another leak. She was one of the two who came to help after the crash. You can even see their similarities." She traced the name below the nurse's photo. "I don't know who Estelle Tavares is, but that's Olena Podrova."

"What? Are you sure?"

Ashley raised a brow at the lieutenant's question.

"I'm sorry. Of course you are. That's great. We didn't have a recent photo of her." He shifted the picture beneath Marko's mug shot.

"Doesn't tie any of them to the cabin, however," Lieutenant Santos said.

"This might." Eden tapped away on her laptop. "Caleb Flynn was adopted at age seven by a Clarissa and Ustov Tarova."

"Russian or Ukrainian background?" Simone murmured.

"Both parents are deceased but Clarissa's maiden name was Wellington. Her father, Misha Wellington, is listed as the purchasing owner of various properties around the country, including a cabin located on the north end of Lassen National Forest," Eden said. "It's still listed in Clarissa's name."

"Flynn never changed it when she died," Simone added. "Hidden in plain sight."

"Just like he's been." Lieutenant Santos glanced up when two men knocked on the doorframe. Given the suits and stern, strained and defensive expressions, Ashley assumed her FBI statement taker had just arrived. "Agent Baxter. Agent Robeson. We've been expecting you. Where's Agent Flynn?"

"We drove over separately," the older of the two said. "He's on a coffee run. Look, I don't know what Agent Harrison has told you—"

"He's told us more than he's told you," Eden said.

"When was the last time you saw Agent Flynn?" Lieutenant Santos pulled out his phone.

"Ten, fifteen minutes maybe?" Robeson said. "I'm sure he'll be here—"

"No," Simone said as the lieutenant connected with Agent Harrison over the phone. "He won't."

"Agent Harrison? Agent Flynn is a no-show." Santos pinned Baxter under a gaze Ashley was certain she never wanted to be on the receiving end of. "Yes, sir. They're here now…Yes, sir. I guarantee they aren't going anywhere." He clicked off. "Agent Quinn will arrive shortly to question you." Santos gestured to two empty chairs. "In the meantime, why don't you take a seat and we'll fill you in."

"This might be the most toxic coffee I've ever ingested." Eden swirled the muddy concoction in the paper cup as Ashley stared down at her steeping tea. "Hey." Ashley glanced up at the gentle hand on hers. "They'll find him. If there's one thing Cole never does, it's give up."

"Neither does Vince," Simone added as she

joined them. One look at the coffee in Eden's hand had her foregoing the coffee maker and reaching for a bottle of water instead.

"Or Jack," Ashley offered. "Why didn't Sawy— I mean, Slade—tell me?" It was the question she couldn't quit asking herself, mainly because she had no answer.

"He was protecting you. You were in a difficult enough position." Eden retrieved the toy Chloe Ann tossed out of the carrier and handed it back to her. Chloe Ann squealed with glee. "You had enough to worry about without giving him away."

"I wouldn't have."

"He couldn't take that chance." Simone sat next to Ashley. "Undercover assignments are some of the toughest in law enforcement. There never seems to be a right answer, only the best one. At the time."

"Oh, I know all about undercover work." Ashley tried to focus on the baby. "My ex-husband spent most of our marriage pretending to be someone else."

"Is that a metaphor or was he actually under-cover?" Eden asked in her usual frank tone.

"Both," Ashley admitted.

"You and Slade spent a lot of time alone. Did you tell him about your ex?"

"Yes." She'd told him just about everything. And yet…had anything he'd told her been true?

"Another reason he probably didn't tell you. Nothing like proving you have a type." Eden flashed a grin at an admonishing Simone. "What? It's kinda true, right?"

Ashley leaned her elbows on the table, covered her face. "She's right. I do have a type. The type that seems determined to lie."

"I'm sure Slade wanted to tell you the truth. Can't speak to your ex-husband, though." Simone took a long drink of her water.

Eden toasted them with her coffee.

"Ashley, there's no use trying to sort out your feelings for Slade at this point. There's still a lot we don't know," Simone said. "Give it some time. Give him the opportunity to explain."

"If he has the chance to." Ashley couldn't explain it, but she knew, she knew, this wasn't going to turn out the way anyone wanted—or expected. "You're right. There's no use dwelling on what I can't change or worrying about what might. I just want the chance to work it all out." With Slade. One way or the other.

"Hey." Cole joined them. "I need to head out. Eden, you going home soon?"

"No. But don't worry," Eden added when Cole's brow furrowed. Investigating cold cases around the country had earned her serious respect from law enforcement, even if she wasn't a cop. "Greta and Allie are taking Chloe Ann until this plays out tonight. This isn't any place for you, is it?" She leaned over and tweaked Chloe Ann's nose.

Cole chuckled.

Eden turned in her chair. "Where are you heading exactly? Back to the port?"

Port? Why would he be headed to the port?

"Ah, no. We have a body reported out at McClellan. Whoever called it in said it matches the description of one of the escapees."

"Sawyer?" Ashley jumped to her feet. The chair clanged to the floor behind her. "Is it—"

"I'm sure if it was, Cole wouldn't have presented the news in this way, would you, Cole?" Simone rested a hand on Ashley's arm.

"I want to come with you." Ashley took a step forward.

Cole shook his head. "No, you don't, Ashley. I'll let you know—"

"Let me rephrase that." Ashley barely gave him a glance as she stalked to the elevators. "I'm coming with you."

"You should wait in the car." Cole pulled his SUV to a stop just in front of the crime scene tape. She could see flashes going off in the near distance.

"I'm getting really tired of people telling me what to do." Ashley shoved out of the door, welcoming the cool air. Night had dropped its curtain over the valley. The airplane hangar was located at the far end of the former air force base.

The uniformed police officer, a young woman standing at attention, held up her hands as they approached.

"It's all right," Cole called from behind Ashley. "Detective Cole Delaney. She's with me."

"Yes, sir."

Cole held up the tape for Ashley to pass under. "Has the coroner arrived yet?"

"On the way, sir. Forensics has begun their evidence collection. I was told to watch for the detective in charge."

"That would be me. Are you first on scene, Officer...?"

"Clarke, sir. Serena Clarke. And yes, sir. I arrived approximately thirty-two minutes ago. As soon as I saw his face, I called in to Major Crimes." She hesitated. "That was the correct procedure, was it not, sir?"

"Absolutely. Walk us over."

"Sir. Ma'am." Officer Clarke gave Ashley a nod of acknowledgment and led the way over to the cruiser. "A caller reported the body, but wasn't on scene when I arrived. As soon as possible, I'd like to search the area for her."

"Noted," Cole said. "We'll get you some additional officers to help with that."

"Appreciated, sir."

"What branch of the military did you serve in, Clarke?"

Ashley found the small talk distracting, in a helpful way. It also sounded as a sharp reminder that life went on. Even when it stopped for some.

"Marines, sir. Finished my second tour in Afghanistan and applied to the department. Six months in."

"Career plans?" Cole pointed and Ashley followed. She hugged her arms around her waist as she went where she was guided.

"Detective, sir."

"That's it? No desire for leadership?"

"No, sir. On the ground. That's where I belong." They stopped short of the spotlighted scene.

"It's not him." Ashley felt her head go light. She'd hoped, she'd prayed, it wasn't. She'd thought Simone was right when she'd said Cole wouldn't have broken that news to her in such a way, but until this moment, she hadn't been sure.

"Ma'am?"

"This is Dr. Ashley McTavish, Officer. She's helping us apprehend the escaped convicts."

"Glad to see you're all right, ma'am."

"Thanks." Ashley managed a quick smile.

"Any idea who it is?" Cole asked.

"It's Badger." Ashley moved forward, careful not to get in the way of the forensics team. "Elliot." Sympathy swarmed as she crouched, examined the body. He'd died quickly and probably unexpectedly. Thanks to all the light, she could see at least two bullet holes, one in his upper spine, the other in the back of his head. "Didn't see it coming, did you, Elliot?"

"Valeri's cleaning house," Cole said. "He wasn't needed anymore."

Nausea churned in her belly. "Last I saw of him, he was driving Valeri away from the cabin. He was eager. Excitable." Whatever else he might have been, he'd also been human. For that alone, he deserved a moment of her grief.

She could only wish that was where her grief would end.

Chapter 15

"You're no Dr. McTavish." A thick gray haze outlined Slade's vision. Javi didn't bother to remove the bullet that was wedged in Slade's shoulder and that turn of luck felt good. He didn't like the idea of anyone, not even ATF Agent Javi, operating on him in the moment.

Instead, Javi cut through Slade's shirt, used the shirt to cover the wound, then wrapped his arm and shoulder in gauze. "You stay with me," Javi whispered.

Taras and Valeri were at the front of the van, close to Olena as she whipped down and around side roads driving toward the West Sacramento Port. What he could expect when they arrived there, other than the presence of Edik Valeri, was anyone's guess.

"Lucky?" Javi gave him a good shake that sent arrows of agony shooting through his body. Oh, man. He was not in good shape.

"Still breathing." But for how much longer? He was sure he had a few cracked ribs, maybe even broken. He also knew his face had taken a beating and he had a headache that would topple a professional boxer. "Any plan?"

"Stay alive?"

"Dude." Slade had to laugh at Javi's mock optimism. "Not helping."

"So, you and the doc."

"Me and the doc. Don't let her hear you call her that, though." What Slade wouldn't give to hear Ashley's voice again, even if it were to berate him for using her well-earned title.

"You keep focused on her. She's a good reason to live."

She was. He'd always suspected when he fell for his soulmate, it would be quick, fast and for life. Sometimes being proved correct was painful in its own right. He'd never met anyone like her, never would again. That combination of wit and smarts and defiance in the face of overwhelming odds, how could he not have fallen in love with her?

"Georgiana," Slade whispered.

"What about her?"

Slade shook his head, unable to dislodge the darkness that seemed to be closing in. "I need you to promise me." He grabbed Javi's shoulder. "Promise me you'll find her. Promise me you'll get her home."

"You can do it your—"

"Promise me." The words ground out of his raw throat. "I'll believe you, Javi. Promise me you'll find her and I'll know she'll be safe again. I can't take that with me."

After a moment, Javi nodded. "I'll find her, brother."

The van screeched to a halt.

Javi sat back. The van fell silent.

Slade could hear the water lapping against the dock. He sat up, blinked quickly to focus out the windshield as Valeri texted on his cell. A few moments later, a light flashed in the distance.

"There." Valeri pointed, but when Olena reached to start the van again, Valeri stopped her. He looked over his shoulder. "Out. We walk from here."

"Awesome," Slade groaned. "I could use some fresh air."

"You and Ashley so deserve each other." Javi grinned and grabbed Slade's uninjured arm and slung it over his shoulders. "We're almost at the end of this journey, partner." Javi's statement, made under his breath, bolstered Slade's flagging energy. "Just a little while longer and it'll all be over."

"Jack is never going to forgive me." Cole slammed his car into Park. "First I take you to a crime scene, now I'm bringing you into the middle of this...whatever it is."

"Jack is well aware of how difficult I can be." Ashley gave him a quick smile. "Don't worry. I'll make him understand."

"You can try," Cole muttered. "Seriously, Ashley. You don't belong here."

She looked at the trailer. This was their command center? "I belong wherever Slade is. However this ends, I need to be there."

"Well, on the bright side, we'll have a doctor on call. Get out. Quietly. We're trying not to bring too much attention—"

A sudden rap on the window had Ashley jumping. She stifled the yelp of surprise before it escaped. Looking out Cole's window, she spotted Eamon.

Cole clicked his key and lowered the window. "Thought you were questioning Baxter."

Eamon shrugged. "Didn't take as long as expected. Both he and Robeson were blindsided by the information about Flynn. Probably saw their careers disappearing when I filled them in. Just got word from Harrison that a van's pulled up on the west side of the docks. Vince is the closest so he's moving into position. Ashley." Eamon shook his head. "Really wish I could say I'm surprised to see you. You here for Jack?"

Cole rolled his head against the back of the seat.

"Sure." Despite the dozens of questions swirling

in her brain, most of them revolving around Slade, she added, "I also thought maybe you could use a medical professional."

"Jack's right," Cole muttered. "You're a terrible liar. We'll follow you in, Eamon."

Shivering, Ashley hurried to keep up with them as they headed to the construction trailer. That her brother was the one to pop the door open to welcome her wasn't a surprise. The expression on his face, however…

"What are you doing here, Ash?" He reached out, grabbed her arm and hauled her in, wrapping her in a hug so tight she could feel his heart pounding. "Man, you scared me."

She fought him at first, wanting to know what was going on with Slade, but when Jack held on, she found herself holding back tears. "I'm okay," she whispered. She didn't realize how much she'd needed this until now. "I'm okay, Jack."

"I'm not." But he finally let go. "Ashley, you shouldn't be here."

Were they all reading from the same script? "I'm not leaving. Not until I know Slade's all right."

Jack opened his mouth, then caught Cole and Eamon shaking their heads at him. "Right. Okay. Better to keep an eye on you, anyway. This is as far as you go, Ash. Don't leave this trailer—you hear me?"

"You couldn't boss me around when we were growing up. You can't boss me around now." But she did understand. She wouldn't leave. Unless she had to.

"Agent Harrison." Jack steered her around the agents buzzing about the claustrophobic trailer.

"Dr. MacTavish."

Ashley had to look up to meet Agent Harrison's gaze. He was a big man, imposing, but not intimidating. He'd rolled his white shirtsleeves up, his tie was askew, and his face carried a concern and level of attention that eased her mind about Slade. A bit. "Please tell me what's going on?"

If he had any qualms about briefing a civilian, he didn't show it. "We caught sight of a van pulling in next to a building at the west end of the docks. No one's emerged yet, but heat signatures indicate at least five people inside."

"Can I see the van?" She indicated the bank of monitors stacked one on top of another.

"Over here." A female agent pointed to the screen above her head.

She recognized the vehicle instantly. "That's the van that showed up after the crash."

"Driven by Olena Podrova and Taras Valeri?" Harrison asked.

"Yes."

"Elliot Handleman is confirmed dead," Cole stated. "Shot twice. He never saw it coming."

"Tying up loose ends. We need ears on that area now," Harrison ordered his people. "We're spread out pretty thin. Weren't sure which direction they were coming from."

"What was that?" Eamon pointed at the screen that showed part of the open water. "A flash of light. Anyone else see it?"

"Got it." The same female agent grabbed the screenshot, pulled it up on her computer. She readjusted the brightness and contrast and shed some light on the boat in the distance.

"Can you clean that up? I see figures out on the deck. Any way to see faces?" Harrison leaned in.

"Working on it, sir." Another few taps on the computer and Ashley and the others also leaned in over the woman's shoulder. "No pressure," the agent whispered to herself. "That's the best I can do."

"It's good enough." Harrison grabbed his radio. "All units, prepare to move in. We have confirmation on Edik Valeri. Moving in off the west dock. Chatter to a minimum. You wait for my go."

Ashley's pulse hammered as the units reported in. Five, six, seven teams of federal agents ready to go at a moment's notice.

"They're getting out of the car." Jack moved in behind Ashley. "Tell us who you recognize, Ash."

"Olena, obviously." She gestured to the only woman in the group circling around the front of the van. "There, that's Taras and Marko. I should have made his stitches tighter." She couldn't believe how well he was moving. "And that's…

Javi." She peered closer as Javi seemed to be struggling.

"He's pulling someone else out with him," Cole said.

Ashley's lungs froze at the sight of Sawyer—Slade—slumping out of the car. Even in the dim light she could see he was bloodied and bruised. "He's been hurt." The sight of the makeshift bandage on his shoulder sent her reeling.

"This time you aren't helping." Jack squeezed reassuring hands on her shoulders. "Not yet."

Harrison clicked his radio again. "All units, report in."

Ashley didn't understand the information that came over the line. All she could do was watch in growing horror as Javi seemed to be half dragging Slade with him. She reached up, squeezed her brother's hands. "Something's wrong," she whispered as the light from the boat backlit the scene. The group headed toward the edge of the dock. "I can feel it. Something's wrong. There!" She pointed to Valeri, who was pulling something out from beneath the back of his shirt.

"She's right," Eamon said. "This is about to go sideways again. Slade needs to know we're here. Can we signal him?"

Harrison held up his hand, eyes pinned to the screen. The entire trailer had gone silent or maybe it was that Ashley couldn't hear anything other than the sound of her own breathing. "Tactical Seven, do you have eyes on Agent Palmer?"

"Sir. In my sights."

"One flash. Make it quick."

"Sir."

"All units?" Harrison scanned the screens. "On my go."

Slade, barely able to feel his legs any longer, leaned heavily on Javi as three shadowy figures emerged up the ladder onto the dock. Marko stood waiting for the trio, gun in hand, Olena and Taras on either side of him, as if awaiting the arrival of their king.

The chilled air this close to the water cleared his mind just enough to watch Edik Valeri, tailored suit, expensive Italian loafers and slicked-back hair that shone against the too-few harbor lights, step forward.

The moment he'd been waiting for. Slade would have sighed in relief if he had any breath to spare. All the months, all the pain and lies and all the waiting coalesced. It wasn't over. Not yet. Not until both Valeri brothers were in custody.

"You disappoint me, Marko." Edik's voice carried a much thicker accent. The smile on the older Valeri's face cut Slade down to the marrow of his bones. Edik held out his arms and embraced his brother. The hearty slap on the back echoed into the night.

Slade scanned their surroundings as Javi carefully, slowly inched them farther out of the brothers' line of sight. Had Baxter gotten the message Slade hid in Clive's jumpsuit? Did he and Javi have backup or were they on their own?

A blink of red flashed along the roofline of the harbor office. Quick. So quick that he wondered if he'd imagined it. Javi tightened his arm, the message clear. He'd seen it. The question was, had anyone else?

"That's one really messed-up family reunion," Javi muttered as Edik hugged his son and then Olena.

"Things did not go completely according to plan." Marko clasped his brother's arms. "But we made it nonetheless. And with a gift. Your very own federal agent."

"Only one?" Edik turned, and even from this distance, Slade knew what was coming next. "How is that possible when I see two before me?"

Javi swore and inched them back another few steps.

"Two?" Marko swung around.

Olena pushed toward Javi, but Marko held out his arm, keeping her behind him.

Taras lifted his weapon.

"I'm sorry to do this to you," Javi whispered.

"Do what?" Slade's foot slipped back and found nothing but air. "Javi—"

"Take a deep breath, brother. We're going in."

As if in slow motion, Slade watched Marko and Taras fire their weapons. But it was Marko who went down, shot by his brother.

Bullets whizzed over Slade's head as he fell back, and then down, down, the air whooshing out of his lungs as he landed hard in the water. Javi's hold on him slipped.

The cold closed over Slade, and he thought of the lake. But the image was gone too quickly, the water now suffocating him. He tried to move, tried to keep up, but his limbs were too heavy.

His mind fogged. The gray hovering in his eyes faded to black. *Ashley. I'm sorry, Ashley. I wish... I wish...*

And he felt himself sink.

"All agents, go. Go! Go! Go!" Harrison yelled into the radio before he shoved himself through the scramble of agents and dived out of the trailer.

"Slade." Ashley moved in close to the monitor, pressed her fingers against the scene where he'd been moments ago. Chaos exploded along with lights as a figure raced out of sight. Olena. Anger boiled in Ashley's stomach.

Another shot rang out and took down Taras. Edik and his bodyguards held up their hands, and were forced to their knees by the swarming officers and agents. "Jack?" Ashley could barely find her voice. "Slade? Where's Slade?"

"You should stay here..."

She swung on him, eyes blazing. "He needs medical attention."

"We have EMTs on standby, Ashley," Cole said.

"She can come with me." Eamon tossed her an FBI windbreaker. "Put this on."

She did so as she ran behind him, adrenaline surging through her system. "He won't last long in that water!" she yelled at Eamon's back. If Slade survived the fall at all. Eamon ran along the edge of the dock, ripping off his jacket, tossed his badge, gun and cell phone to the ground. He didn't hesitate before diving into the water where Javi and Slade had been only moments before.

Ashley picked up Eamon's things, tucked them into her pockets and she scooped up his jacket as additional agents joined her at the edge of the dock.

"Ashley, stay back." Jack hollered at the team. "Lights! We need lights over here! Agent down!"

Spotlights exploded from the two watercraft racing toward them. A helicopter swooped in overhead, with a searchlight scanning the water.

"There!" Ashley shouted when she spotted Javi struggling toward the surface. But where was Slade? And Eamon? She looked for any sign, any sight... A hand burst from the surface and grabbed hold of the metal ladder. "Eamon." She pointed and shouted. "He's there. There!" As Eamon's head bobbed above the water, she saw him straining to drag Slade's unmoving form with him. "Help him!" But she hadn't needed to say anything. Two agents had already climbed down, propped themselves on either side of the ladder and were reaching out to haul both of them up.

"Back up, Ashley. Give them room."

She heard sirens in the distance, but they'd be too late. "Here! Put him here!" She swept her hair back and dropped to her knees as the two agents lowered Slade onto the ground.

Her hands landed on his chest instantly, pumping, pumping water out, pumping air in. His face was pale, his body motionless. "Don't you die on me, Slade Palmer. Not until you explain yourself. Don't." Another pump. "You." Another pump. "Die!"

She stopped long enough to plug his nose and breathe into his mouth. She knew she should keep pumping, but she needed him to breathe. She resumed the chest compressions, felt Jack and Cole at her back as if closing ranks. "Not today." She pumped again and again. "Not today…not today."

"Ashley." Jack bent down, but she shoved him off. "Ashley—"

Slade sputtered and coughed. He was choking in air as he blinked and moved his head from side to side. Confusion filled his eyes. His breathing sounded horrible, as if he still had half the harbor in his lungs. "Slade." She tried to push him onto his side, but he was too big and too injured. His hand flailed out, fingers flexing as if searching for something. "I've got you." She grabbed his hand, held it against her chest and leaned over him. "Slade? Hey there. Yeah. That's it. Look at me." She smoothed his hair back, leaned over him. "You see me? Can you see me, Slade?"

He nodded. "Ash-Ashley." His voice sounded raw. Scraped. Beautiful. "I'm alive?"

"Oh, yeah, you are." Tears clouded her vision. "And you have a lot of explaining to do."

"Yeah. Javi." He tried to look to the side. "Did they find—"

"They've got him." Jack bent down, covered Slade's and Ashley's hands with his own. "You did good, Slade. You did real good."

"Jack," Slade managed to whisper. "Good. Home."

"Yes. You got me home." Ashley couldn't stop crying.

"Javi," Slade murmured as his eyes fluttered closed. "Get—agent. AT…" His head lolled to the side and he passed out.

The EMTs slid into place, leaving Ashley feeling helpless as Jack dragged her away. "He can't die. I won't let him," Ashley told her brother and Cole as they encircled her.

"Something tells me he won't. Did you hear him? Javi's ATF?"

"I heard," Cole said. Together, the three of them turned to watch Eamon reaching out a hand to help haul Javi onto the dock.

"That was some dive, definitely a ten-point-oh,"

Jack teased Eamon as the soaking wet agent approached them.

"Swim team in college." Eamon huffed. "Been a long time since then. You good, Ash?"

Ashley nodded and, before she could stop herself, she threw her arms around him.

"It's over, Ash." Eamon returned the embrace and gave her an extra squeeze. "It's all over."

"No, it's not." Agent Harrison joined them. Over his shoulder, Ashley could see federal agents leading Edik and his two bodyguards away.

"What do you mean?" Cole asked.

"Olena," Ashley whispered as the EMTs loaded Slade onto a stretcher. "Olena got away."

Chapter 16

"Ash? Hey, Ash."

Ashley shot up, pulled out of the sleep she hadn't realized she'd fallen into. She straightened in her chair. "What is it? Is it Slade? Is he—" She looked around the hospital room—not dissimilar to the one she'd occupied earlier—and found Slade in the bed, his monitors beeping steadily.

"There's no change yet. I was worried you were about to fall out of that seat." Jack took the chair next to hers.

She sagged against Jack's shoulder, exhaustion creeping up again.

"I'd tell you to go home, get some sleep there, but I'm guessing that won't happen."

She shook her head. "I'm not leaving until he's awake."

"Figured." Morning had come and gone and with it, most of her energy and thinking ability. She only remembered talking to the doctors after Slade got out of surgery. Aside from the second bullet wound in his shoulder, he had three broken ribs, a ruptured spleen, a broken nose and a mild concussion, probably from when he'd hit the water. He was, her medical brain knew, lucky to be alive. "Greta's going to stop by later with something to eat. Everyone else is anxious to see you, but I suggested we wait until you're feeling better."

"I feel fine." Just drained, physically and emotionally, and feeling very, very confused. "How's Javi?"

"Remarkably fine. Bullet grazed him. If he hadn't taken that dive when he did, different story."

"I can't believe there were two federal agents in that cabin with me." Then again, considering Javi had thrown her that phone—a lifeline to her brother—maybe she could.

"They're both pretty good at their jobs." Jack patted her hand. "How are you really feeling, Ash? About Slade."

She turned her head and looked at Slade, the broken, bruised man who had slipped his way into her heart. "I love him. So much that it hurts."

"Enough to put up with his job?"

She shrugged. Her throat tightened, because he wasn't asking her something she hadn't been asking herself. "It's a part of him. If I love him, I have to love all of him. Even the parts that scare me."

"You didn't do so well with Adam."

"Adam was not a good man." Ashley huffed and earned a grin from her brother. "I didn't love Adam. I mean…well, yeah, I guess I did. But I was never in love with him. I know what that feels like now. As if I'm not whole if he's not with me. That sounds silly, doesn't it?" She leaned her chin in her hand.

"It's not stupid at all. How do you think I feel about Greta?"

Ashley laughed. "I know how you feel about her. You're totally in love." And it thrilled her a tiny bit to know she had the potential for that in her own life now. "Have I ever got some stuff to figure out. I still haven't given my official statement."

"Eamon said he'd come get it here."

"That's the second-best thing I've heard all day." Her gaze flicked to the TV screen in the corner. "Have they found her?"

"Olena? Not yet. I'd say she won't get far but…"

"She's a chameleon." Ashley sighed. "Or some kind of other lizard. She just slithered away." She snapped her fingers. "Just like that. Gone. Creepy."

"Yeah, well, we'll find her. There isn't grass tall enough to hide her forever."

Ashley caught a movement out of the corner of her eye. "Javi! What are you doing here?"

"Came to check up on him. And you. No, stay there." He waved her back down when she started to stand. "You've had a rough week."

Ashley couldn't help but stare at him. She'd never noticed how good-looking he was. Dark hair, dark eyes. Maybe she'd just been blinded by Slade from the start. Or maybe Javi was as much as a chameleon as Olena in the looks department.

"Case closed?" Jack asked.

Javi shrugged. "It's complicated. ATF and FBI are fighting over jurisdiction. We've also got Interpol involved, but it'll work itself out. I have the information I wanted from Edik, at least." He stood over Slade and stared down at him, saying, "I'm going to be gone for a bit. Something I have to take care of."

"You're coming back, aren't you?" Ashley didn't like the idea of his vanishing out of her life.

"I'll be back." Javi tossed her a smile. "I've got a promise to keep. Take care, Ashley. You, too, Jack."

"Wonder what that was about?" Jack wondered out loud once Javi left.

Ashley had an idea, but she remained silent. That was one thing she didn't want to be wrong about.

"You want me to ask them to bring in a cot for you so you can get some actual sleep?"

"No, I'm good." She claimed his seat when he got up, then settled her feet on her chair. "If you see Eamon, tell him to wake me up. I want to get that statement over with sooner rather than later." She snuggled back down, braced her head on her arm. "And if Greta's taking orders, I'd love some mac and cheese."

* * *

When Ashley awoke again, it was dark. Someone had come in and turned on the light above Slade, drawn the curtain around the bed for privacy. She blinked, not quite unsettled, but the nerves remained nonetheless.

She unfolded herself out of the chair, groaning and straining and regretting instantly that she hadn't had Jack ask for that cot. Maybe it was Eamon behind the curtain with Slade. She'd assumed he would have shown up by now. That hadn't happened yet.

After downing a bottle of water and using the bathroom, she pushed back the curtain but it was only Slade she saw. She looked him over and wondered when he was going to pull himself out of the darkness and come back to her. She knew she was asking for too much, too soon, but that didn't mean she wouldn't ask.

She smoothed a hand down the side of his face and considered if he would shave at some point. She wasn't entirely sure she wanted him to. She liked the ragged, rugged look to him. But having seen his official FBI photo, she had to give that version a chance. If he was going to give her one.

All this time she'd been trying to sort through her own feelings, about her own future. What if he didn't feel the same way? What if everything between them had been nothing more than the role he was playing? She had to take things slow. They had, after all, only known each other for a matter of days. Was it very ridiculous for her to be thinking about…forever?

She raised her arms above her head, stretched out more of the kinks. Wanting to move, she headed into the hall, where she introduced herself to the night nurse team. They didn't seem surprised to see her and, luckily, the perks of being a physician in town meant they wouldn't kick her out. Not unless she got in their way. She wasn't planning to, but given how her life had been going lately, who knew?

"Dr. McTavish?" One of the nurses popped out of the break room. "If you're hungry, your sister-in-law dropped off dinner earlier. We've kept it for you in the fridge."

"Thank you so much," Ashley said gratefully. "You just saved me from a vending-machine meal." Although she had been looking forward to those cheese curls. "Can I?" She pointed to the door.

"Of course. Microwave's all yours."

When the wafting aroma of hot cheese reached her nose a few minutes later, Ashley almost sobbed. She had her first mouthful on her way back to Slade. A shadow crossed the hallway and seemed to enter Slade's room. The telltale comfortable shoes the nurse was wearing eased her concern. "He's not due for any medication for a while," Ashley said as she walked into the room and set her dinner down on the table near the plastic pitcher of water. "And his vital signs…" She lifted her gaze to the woman's face, then to the hypodermic needle she had poised to inject into Slade's saline drip. "Olena."

It wasn't a total shock that the woman had slipped past the security the FBI had positioned down the hall. She'd lopped off most of her hair, smoothed it into a pixie cut and coated her eyes with a thick layer of liner and shadow. The rainbow unicorn scrubs added to the facade, as did the pass clipped to the hem of her top.

But the murderous look in her eyes? That was all Olena.

"Your timing has not improved," Olena said. She inched the needle closer.

"Stop, please!" Ashley nearly launched herself toward the bed. "Don't hurt him. Just…don't."

Olena frowned. "This is all I have left to do."

Ashley saw Slade lift a finger, then wait, and raise it again. *Stall*, she told herself. *Keep her talking. Keep her talking until…until what?* "I'm sorry about your father."

"Are you?"

"Well, yes. Everything that's happened has been sad. Lives wasted. So much hurt and pain, and for what? Wealth? Power? Control?" She noticed Olena's look of frustration and knew she couldn't risk losing her attention. "Your dad. He played a good game of chess." Her pulse thudded in her throat. "And I'm guessing he was a passable father."

"He was a horrible father," Olena spit. Her hand jerked. "But he was all I had." She tilted her chin up. "And he should have killed you on the bus."

"He almost did." Slade raised his hand an inch, maybe more. The movement was steady, strong even. Olena focused on the open door; there were noises in the hallway. Agents? The police? Someone who could help, Ashley hoped. She couldn't risk looking at him. Couldn't risk Olena seeing. "Killing Slade won't bring your father back."

"I know that," Olena snapped. "This isn't about bringing him back. It's about finishing what should have happened. First him. Then you."

"It makes no sense." Ashley stepped closer to the bed. The beeping from Slade's monitors grew louder. One of the night nurses stopped just inside the door. Ashley raised her hands, shook her head. "You won't make it out of here alive, Olena. There are FBI agents here." She sneaked a quick look at the nurse, who nodded and vanished down the hall. "They're looking for you."

"Everyone's looking for me." She aligned the tip of the needle with the line. "But they don't see me. They never see me. But you did. Maybe I should kill you first. Put you out of *my* misery."

"You can try." Ashley wasn't ready to die. Knew it down deep in her soul. She'd been through too much to lose everything now. A calm descended.

Olena dropped the syringe on a tall table by Slade's bedside and from behind produced her favorite knife. Ashley recognized it even from where she was standing.

Just as Olena began to move, Slade's hand

whipped up and locked around Olena's wrist. "Now, Ashley!"

She lunged forward, grabbed Olena's shoulders and shoved her backward. Olena cried out. The knife clattered to the floor. Ashley scrambled to retrieve the weapon and, pivoting, held it up to Olena's throat once she had it.

Slade dropped back onto the bed. His eyes were closed, his expression free of worry. The corners of his mouth tipped up.

Ashley stood there, shook her head when Olena eyed the vacant doorway. It was vacant only for a moment, as Eamon, Jack, Cole and half a dozen other agents flooded into the room.

She handed off the knife to her brother and walked to Slade's side. She kissed him before he had a chance to speak. Before he had a chance to think. And when she felt his hand move to the back of her neck, slip into her hair, she knew…whatever else might happen, as long as she had Slade by her side, she was going to be okay.

Epilogue

Two months later...

It was coming together, Slade thought as he knocked the last railing into place. The new porch was only the latest addition to his recent purchase, a purchase he'd been able to make thanks to Don Harrison. The SAC had tracked down the ownership records of the cabin that only a few months earlier had protected Ashley's life and Slade's.

The fresh coat of exterior paint had taken him longer than expected, more than four weekends, but then, he still wasn't moving as well as he'd have liked. His physical therapy was progressing, but he enjoyed the added exertion, especially when it was on the cabin where he had fallen in love with Ashley.

"You ready for a beer?" Agent Eamon Quinn emerged from inside the cabin, bottle in hand. "Or are you waiting for Ashley to get back?"

He accepted the bottle greedily. "Thanks for coming up to help. I couldn't have gotten that new gas line installed alone."

"Always happy to take a break from the agency." Eamon leaned against the frame as Slade put away his tools. "Speaking of the agency, you decide what you're going to do? That early retirement they offered you isn't a bad deal."

"No, it's not." The deal was no doubt an effort to make up for the fact that a corrupt FBI agent—the only one of Valeri's crew to remain at large—had nearly ended his and a lot of other people's lives. "But I'm not ready to retire. I've asked them about teaching. I'd like to come up with a special training course for undercover agents. Maybe Quantico, maybe traveling around. Not too much, though. I want to stay close to home."

Eamon nodded. "Don't blame you. This cabin is going to be a great weekend getaway for you two. You get all your stuff moved into her place?"

"Finally." They still had about a dozen boxes to unpack, but for the first time in a long time, he felt settled. It didn't hurt he had a knockout doctor taking very good care of him. "Don't suppose you're going to tell me what's in store for my bachelor party?"

"Nope." Eamon grinned and drank his beer. "Jack and Max are having a great time planning it, though."

"Never thought I'd have my future brother-in-law planning my bachelor party. That's usually the best man's job."

"I surrendered the task as soon as I found out he really wanted to do it. I know when to get out of the way." Eamon laughed. "Where is Ashley, anyway? Wedding stuff?"

"She, too, has surrendered. Greta's overseeing all that. Ashley and I would have been happy eloping but—"

"Ha. No way you're chickening out of the celebration." Eamon toasted him. "We're all way too invested in your welcome into the family. You can come up here and hide afterward for the honeymoon."

Exactly how Slade planned it. The rumble of an engine coming along the now-cleared road had them both straightening. "Ashley?" Eamon asked.

"That's not her car." The dark SUV pulled up at the front porch. "But it's her." Ashley jumped out of the SUV the second it stopped. "Company?" he called to her.

"You could say that." Ashley ran right up to him and planted a kiss on his lips. "Surprise!"

"What's the surprise?" He slipped his arm around her and watched as Javi climbed out from behind the steering wheel. "Well, it's about time you turned up," he said, grinning, to the ATF agent. He let Ashley go long enough to shake his friend's hand. "Just in time for the wedding. Where've you been?"

"Fulfilling a promise." Javi took a step and opened the back door. The young woman who stepped down was as beautiful and as alive as he remembered.

"Georgiana." He swayed and Ashley held him tight. "But…how…?" He opened his arms. Georgiana filled them as much as Ashley filled his heart. "You're okay…you're okay."

She nodded, sobbing, hugging him. "I knew you'd find me." Slade felt like hollering for joy. "I knew it. I never gave up hope."

"Javi found you." He pressed his lips to the top of his cousin's head, reached out a hand to Ashley, who was wiping away tears of her own.

"It was thanks to you, though."

"Your mom? Does Aunt Vicki know?" he asked.

Georgiana nodded. "We stopped for a few days before coming here. I thought about waiting until it got closer to the wedding, but Ashley insisted."

Ashley. He sighed. "You knew? How long?" he asked her.

"Not long." Ashley winked. "So. You really gonna marry me, Lucky?"

"That I am." He brought her into the hug. "That I am indeed."

* * * * *

Missed Eden's story? Or Simone's?
For more romantic suspense
from Anna J. Stewart,
visit www.Harlequin.com today!

#2171 SNOWED IN WITH A COLTON
The Coltons of Colorado • by Lisa Childs

Certain her new guest at the dude ranch she co-owns is hiding something, Aubrey Colton fights her attraction to him. Luke Bishop is hiding something—his true identity: Luca Rossi, an Italian journalist on the run from the mob.

#2172 CAVANAUGH JUSTICE: THE BABY TRAIL
Cavanaugh Justice • by Marie Ferrarella

Brand-new police detective partners Korinna Kennedy and Brodie Cavanaugh investigate a missing infant case and uncover a complicated conspiracy while Korinna is slowly drawn into Brodie's life and family—causing her to reevaluate her priorities in life.

#2173 DANGER AT CLEARWATER CROSSING
Lost Legacy • by Colleen Thompson

After his beloved twins are returned from the grandparents who've held them for years, widowed resort owner Mac Hale-Walker finds his long-anticipated reunion threatened by a beautiful social worker sent to assess his fitness to parent—and a plot to forcibly separate him from his children forever.

#2174 TROUBLE IN BLUE
Heroes of the Pacific Northwest • by Beverly Long

Interim police chief Marcus Price is captivated by newcomer Erin McGarry, who has come to Knoware to help her sick sister. But he has his hands full with a string of robberies and a credible terrorist threat, and he's not confident that Erin didn't bring the danger to the small community or that either one of them will survive it.

SPECIAL EXCERPT FROM

ⓗ HARLEQUIN

ROMANTIC SUSPENSE

Interim police chief Marcus Price is captivated by newcomer Erin McGarry, who has come to Knoware to help her sick sister. But he has his hands full with a string of robberies and a credible terrorist threat, and he's not confident that Erin didn't bring the danger to the small community or that either one of them will survive it.

Read on for a sneak preview of
Trouble in Blue,
the next thrilling romance in Beverly Long's Heroes of the Pacific Northwest series!

Marcus watched as she got to her feet. He was grateful to see that she was steady.

"Can we have a minute?" Marcus asked Blade.

"Yeah. Hang on to her good arm," his friend replied. Then he walked away, taking Dawson with him.

"What?" she asked, offering him a sweet smile.

"I'm going to find who did this. I promise you. And you're going to be okay. Jamie Weathers is the best emergency physician this side of the Colorado River. Hell, this side of the Missouri River. He'll fix you up. But don't leave the hospital until you hear from me. You understand?"

HRSEXP0122B

"I got it," she said. "I'm going to be fine. It's all going to be fine. I barely had twenty bucks in my bag. He didn't even get my phone. I had that in my back pocket. Nor my keys. Those were in my hand. So he basically got nothing except the cash and my driver's license."

Things didn't matter. "You want me to let Brian and Morgan know?"

"Oh, God, no. Please don't do that." She looked panicked. "Morgan can't have stress right now. I'm grateful that her room is on the other side of the building. Otherwise, she could be watching this spectacle."

They would want to know. But it was her decision. And she was in pain. "Okay," he said, giving in easily.

"Thank you," she said.

"Go get fixed up. I'll talk to you soon."

She nodded.

"And, Erin…" he added.

"Yeah."

"I'm really glad that you're okay."

Don't miss
Trouble in Blue *by Beverly Long,*
available March 2022 wherever
Harlequin Romantic Suspense
books and ebooks are sold.

Harlequin.com

Get 4 FREE REWARDS!

We'll send you 2 FREE Books plus 2 FREE Mystery Gifts.

Harlequin Romantic Suspense books are heart-racing page-turners with unexpected plot twists and irresistible chemistry that will keep you guessing to the very end.

FREE
Value Over
$20
